Fallen Angel

MARTY HOLLAND

Introduction by
Curtis Evans

Stark House Press • Eureka California

FALLEN ANGEL

Published by Stark House Press
1315 H Street
Eureka, CA 95501, USA
griffinskye3@sbcglobal.net
www.starkhousepress.com

FALLEN ANGEL
Copyright © 1945 by Marty Holland and published by E. P. Dutton &
Company Inc., New York; and Peter Davies, London, 1946. Reprinted in a
revised & updated version in paperback as *Blonde Baggage*, Avon, 1949.

Reprinted by permission of Suzanne Estella Tarvin. All rights reserved
under International and Pan-American Copyright Conventions.

"The Mystery Lady of Noir: Marty Holland and her Fallen Angel (1945)"
copyright © 2023 by Curtis Evans

ISBN: 979-8-88601-019-0

Cover and text design by Mark Shepard, shepgraphics.com
Proofreading by Bill Kelly

PUBLISHER'S NOTE:
This is a work of fiction. Names, characters, places and incidents are
either the products of the author's imagination or used fictionally, and
any resemblance to actual persons, living or dead, events or locales, is
entirely coincidental.
Without limiting the rights under copyright reserved above, no part of
this publication may be reproduced, stored, or introduced into a retrieval
system or transmitted in any form or by any means (electronic,
mechanical, photocopying, recording or otherwise) without the prior
written permission of both the copyright owner and the above publisher
of the book.

First Stark House Press Edition: March 2023

FALLEN ANGEL

Eric Stanton is a drifter and a con artist. After he gets kicked off a bus from L.A., he finds himself in the small coastal town of Walton. This is where he meets Stella, a local waitress. She's down on her luck, too, so they make a good pair. So good that Stanton decides to pull a grift on a naïve young woman named Emmie with a large inheritance. Stanton figures that with her $10,000 in his pocket, he and Stella can make a fresh start somewhere else.

What he doesn't figure is that Emmie will actually fall for him. Then Stella is found murdered. And Mark Judd, the cop in charge of the investigation, is getting pretty rough with his interrogations. It'd make anybody sweat. And Stanton is beginning to sweat plenty…

"…a Cain-type portrait of a heel."
—*Richmond Times-Dispatch*

Marty Holland Bibliography

Novels
Fallen Angel (Dutton, 1945; revised & updated as
  Blonde Baggage, Avon, 1949; Novel Library, 1950)
The Glass Heart (Julian Messner, 1946; reprinted as
  Her Private Passions, Avon, 1948)
Fast Woman (Diversey, 1949)
Darling of Paris (Avon, 1949)
Baby Godiva (2011; published posthumously)

Novellas
Terror for Two (*Scarab Mystery Magazine*, January 1951)
The Sleeping City (*Thrilling Detective*, Fall 1952)

Short stories
Lady With a Torch (*Thrilling Love*, Oct 1943; as by Mary Holland)
Night Watchman (*The Shadow*, March 1943)
Rain, Rain, Go Away (*The Shadow*, April 1943)
D.O.A.—East River (*Street & Smith's Detective Story Magazine*,
  March 1944)

Screenplays
The File on Thelma Jordon (1950; original story)

7
The Mystery Lady of Noir Marty Holland and Her *Fallen Angel* (1945) by Curtis Evans

17
FALLEN ANGEL
By Marty Holland

The Mystery Lady of Noir
Marty Holland and Her *Fallen Angel* (1945)

by Curtis Evans

For a brief span of years in postwar Hollywood, Mary Hauenstein—a pretty, petite, blue-eyed, fluffily blonde-haired former stenographer at Paramount Pictures who unexpectedly wrote crime fiction under the far snappier, sexually ambiguous nom de plume Marty Holland—was a shining star in the criminal constellation of noir fiction and film. Before *Fallen Angel*, Marty Holland's "tough" debut crime novel, was even published in 1945, the film studio 20th Century Fox eagerly snapped up the screen rights; and the resultant picture of the same name, directed by Otto Preminger and starring the winning acting trio of Dana Andrews, Alice Faye and Linda Darnell, premiered just seven months after the novel. The next year RKO purchased—once again before the book was published—the screen rights to Holland's second crime novel, *The Glass Heart*, intending it to serve as a starring vehicle for crooner turned hard-boiled film star Dick Powell, to be directed by Robert Montgomery and scripted by leading noir novelist James M. Cain—though this project fell though after Montgomery opted for other hard-boiled/noir projects (respectively *The Lady in the Lake* and *Ride the Pink Horse*, based on novels by Raymond Chandler and Dorothy B. Hughes.) Undaunted, Holland in 1948 contributed the story treatment that became the basis for the 1950 Paramount noir crime film *The File on Thelma Jordan*, directed by Robert Siodmak and starring noir veteran Barbara Stanwyck in the title role. While admittedly small, Marty Holland's criminal legacy is by no means insignificant, yet in the Fifties and Sixties the author faded into obscurity in a remarkably thorough disappearing act which the years after her death in 1971 did nothing to alleviate until 2016, when in the *Los Angeles Review of Books* writer Sarah Weinman published an article, "The Hollywood Ladies of Serie Noire," that was partly about Holland. In her article Weinman surveyed Holland's achievements and pointedly lamented "the ease with which culture forgets about women in the creative arts." Now, seven years later, Marty Holland has finally returned to print in the United States with a new edition of Holland's *Fallen Angel* published by Stark House, one publisher that seemingly never forgets.

Even after the publication of Weinman's article, however, Marty Holland has remained noir's mystery woman, with most of her past seeming forever fated to stay uncompromisingly murky. "Things go blank," declared a stymied Weinman in her article concerning Holland's pre-Paramount years. One of the few known "facts" about Marty Holland—that she was born Mary Hauenstein in Beaverdam, Ohio in 1919—is partly true. Holland indeed was born Mary Hauenstein in Beaverdam, a tiny agricultural village located near the small city of Lima in northwestern Ohio that over the years has gone from a population of 353 in 1880 to one of 319 in 2020. However, Mary came into the world not in 1919 but rather half-a-dozen years earlier on November 2, 1913.

The woman who became Marty Holland, it turns out, was the youngest of the six children of Beaverdam hardware merchant Albert Hauenstein and his wife Virginia "Vinnie" Shull, a schoolteacher and granddaughter of prominent country doctor and ardent Prohibitionist Jesse Guy Honnell. Albert was the son of Swiss immigrants Johannes and Barbara Hauenstein, a fact which likely explains Holland's striking blonde, blue-eyed good looks, a feature amplified by the "Holland" surname which she would choose for herself. The future author could have passed for the "Pretty Little Dutch Girl" in the nursery rhyme of that title.

The Hauensteins were a farming couple who in addition to crops produced numerous doubtlessly worthy but evidently unremarkable descendants in the Beaverdam area. However sometime during the 1920s Albert and Vinnie migrated with their six children to California, settling in Huntington Park, where

Holland attended high school between 1928 and 1931. At Huntington Park High School the outgoing, effervescent young woman was extremely active in thespianism. In 1929 she performed the female lead role of aspiring young actress Lola Pratt, the lovely "baby-talk girl" who so captivates the ingenuous teenage male protagonist in the stage adaptation of Booth Tarkington's bestselling novel *Seventeen* (Ruth Gordon originated the role on Broadway) and in 1931 she herself directed the student play, demonstrating that she had brains to go along with her looks.

After leaving Huntingdon Park High School, Holland's comely appearance and acting experience may have inclined her to try her luck as an actress in nearby Hollywood, but, in any event, she eventually ended up working as a secretary at Paramount. By the early 1940s, Holland, after having typed so many scripts for crime films, had concluded that she could do better herself, so she daringly quit her job and had at it. At least she had the advantage of being able to do her own typing!

In 1943, as she entered her thirtieth (not her twenty-fourth) year, Holland published a love story, "Lady with a Torch," in the romance pulp *Thrilling Love* and a pair of short stories, "Night Watchman" and "Rain, Rain, Go Away," in the crime pulp *The Shadow*. The next year another short crime tale by her, "D.O.A.—East River," appeared in *Street & Smith's Detective Story Magazine*. For her love story Holland had used the pseudonym Mary Holland, while for her crime tales she kept the Holland surname but changed the decidedly feminine Mary to the decidedly more masculine Marty, the crime pulps in her view being something of an old boy's club.

In one of her rare newspaper interviews Marty Holland avowed that she preferred writing crime tales to love stories because crime plots came easily to her. "[O]nce you've got your plot for a detective story," she drolly declared, "it writes itself….that is, if you spend 14 hours a day helping it along." Having prenticed in the pulps, Holland in 1944 wrote a 56,000-word novel entitled *Fallen Angel*, which later that year was accepted on the very same day by both the publisher E. P. Dutton and the film studio 20th Century Fox, the latter of whom for the screen rights paid the author the whopping sum of $40,000 (about $600,000 today). With her cup of riches suddenly running over, Holland left her job and moved into a fancy Beverly Hills apartment with her older unmarried sister Martha. Surely Holland enjoyed one of the most rapid rises to success of any crime writer up to that time.

In September 1944, nine months before *Fallen Angel* actually went into print with Dutton, newspapers announced that actor Dana Andrews would play the male lead in the film, which Otto Preminger was to direct as the follow-up to his classic mystery movie *Laura*, a critically-acclaimed smash that had paired Andrews with Gene Tierney in the star-making title role. In January 1945, Louella Parsons divulged in her "In Hollywood" column that sultry brunette actress Linda Darnell had been secured as one of the two female leads in the film. Two months later newspapers asserted that Anne Baxter had been cast as the other female lead, but by April this part had been taken on by hugely popular musical star Alice Faye, who after a two-year absence from cinema to raise her baby daughter was eager to return to film in a meaty dramatic role.

In May, Dutton published *Fallen Angel* to generally good reviews, although it was received unenthusiastically by several prominent critics, including Anthony Boucher, who dismissively pronounced the would-be "tough" novel nothing more than "ersatz [James M.] Cain." However many other reviewers were more inclined to lift up *Fallen Angel*, finding nothing of the ersatz in it. In the *Daily Times* of Davenport, Iowa, Addie May Swan lauded the tale as not only "an ingenious novel of crime with a hard-to-guess solution but ... a fascinating character study," while "B.B.J." in the *Richmond Times-Dispatch* marveled: "You wouldn't think a girl who looks as nice as the author of 'Fallen Angel'—her picture is on the jacket—would write such a tough yarn. But Miss Holland has turned in a [James M.] Cain-type portrait of a heel." The unsigned reviewer in the *Cincinnati Post* similarly was struck by the blunt fact of the author's fair sex, observing: "Marty, surprisingly enough, considering the rough language her characters use, is a woman, but she writes convincingly from the male viewpoint. The mystery-loving public will await more of the same from Miss Holland." In England, where *Fallen Angel* was published by Peter Davies, a reviewer for the *Liverpool Echo* was similarly impressed with the toughness of this novice lady author, pithily avowing: "If you like movement, just watch Marty Holland step on the gas."

The film adaptation of *Fallen Angel* premiered on December 14, 1945. For the most part the acting in the picture was highly praised, with laurels going to Linda Darnell as the tale's sexy bad girl and murder victim, although the script frequently was faulted for its implausibility at points. At the *New York Times* film critic Bosley Crowther pronounced that "for all of its acting wealth, 'Fallen Angel' falls short of being a top flight whodunit" and he contrasted the film unfavorably with Otto Preminger's *Laura*, a "taut and superior murder mystery." Today *Fallen Angel*, although acknowledged as no *Laura*, is generally admired in spite of its flaws.

While the film version of *Fallen Angel* has retained no small measure of critical and popular currency among classic crime film fans, the book which inspired it has been largely forgotten. However, Marty Holland's crime novel is of interest not only for its connection to Otto Preminger's film but as an example of a sort of peculiarly feminine noir-romance hybrid. As we have seen, Anthony Boucher derided this quality as ersatz James M. Cain, rightly noting that Holland had adulterated the heady bitterness of Cain, so powerfully evident in such noir landmarks as *The Postman Always Rings Twice* and *Double Indemnity*, with a more saccharine view of human nature; yet happily in the real world the darkness in human nature is in fact frequently relieved by flashes of light, as our better angels take hold. The very title of Holland's novel expresses her view that men and women are redeemable by the benevolent force of love.

The novel and the film open the same way, with drifter and grifter Eric Stanton, the narrator of the novel, getting kicked off a Greyhound bus to San Francisco by the driver, on account of his not having sufficient fare left to cover the final leg of the journey. He is unceremoniously dumped in the dumpy little coastal town of Walton, a conservative backwater filled with pious, churchgoing souls like the highly respectable and well-off Barkley sisters, Emmie and Clara, though among the town's less reputable citizens one finds lovely but crudely mercenary Stella Flint, the waitress at a local grease pit called Pop's. When Eric meets town siren Stella he, like seemingly most of the other men is town, is hit hard by her stunning beauty; but Stella is playing the dating game for keeps—i.e., marriage—and will not waste time on some big talking bum. (Stanton describes beauteous Stella, by the by, thusly: "She was blonde. All frizz. Her hair was short above her ears, fluffed all over her head ... Blue eyes." This description could have matched that of the author herself.)

Stalled by Stella, Eric, being the consummate stinker that he is, starts hatching a plan to satisfy the waitress' ambitions and thereby his own. This involves a visiting spiritualist by the name of Professor Ernest Madley and the prim but soulful Emmie, the younger of the two Barkley girls. (Her sister Clara has written off men for good.) But when Stella gets violently bumped off, Eric ends up placed high on the list of suspects of hotshot visiting New York cop Mark Judd; and he has to play detective himself to avoid getting issued a complimentary ticket to the death house. Whodunit? At times it seems like the answer could be *anyone*. Stella, it seems, was made to be murdered.

With its tense situation and passionate emotional conflicts, it is easy to see the appeal of *Fallen Angel* to director Otto Preminger and producer Darryl F. Zanuck, both of whom were looking to score another smash hit character-driven murder mystery like *Laura*. But *Laura*, authored by Vera Caspary, is really little like *Fallen Angel*, except in its emphasis on the deadly consequences of sexual obsession. *Laura*, both in its book and cinematic forms, is a fabulously sophisticated and witty tale, with posh people moving swankily about in luxury surroundings. The drab small-town California setting of Walton, with its parochial citizens and lowlifes and its dive diner Pop's, really could not be farther from *Laura*'s tony New York penthouse milieu. Even Eric's grand ambition—to bilk the Barkley sisters out of $20,000 (half of what Marty Holland received for the film rights to the novel)—seems utterly small potatoes in comparison with the lavish goings-on in *Laura*. Stella herself, enticing as she is on the surface (especially as incarnated by lovely Linda Darnell), has none of the depth and enigmatic appeal of Caspary's and Preminger's winsome title character Laura. Dana Andrews, who played the tough police investigator and male half of the romantic interest in *Laura*, intensely disliked the role of Eric Stanton in *Fallen Angel* and resisted taking the part, only accepting after being threatened with a studio suspension. One can see why Andrews had distaste for the part, for Eric Stanton for much of the novel is essentially nothing more than a cheap punk. Certainly in *Fallen Angel* Dana Andrews is as compelling as he was in *Laura*, but it is hard to accept him as such an essentially weak character. At thirty-six (and looking older), Andrews also was too old for the part, Eric being a callow twenty-eight. Andrews later freely admitted that "Linda Darnell is the best thing in the picture," and there is some truth to that, although Alice Faye, in the "good girl" role of Eric's steadfast better angel Emmie to my mind has received insufficient due for her understated, subtly moving performance. Noir film critics are a cynical bunch.

Notorious casting couch creep Darryl Zanuck is said to have been responsible, in a bid to deemphasize Alice Faye's role in relation to that of his alleged mistress Linda Darnell, for cutting no fewer than a dozen of Faye's scenes from the film, including one where Faye sings the flick's signature tune "Slowly", which in the film is played repeatedly on the jukebox by Stella. Shocked by seeing the drastic cuts to her part at the first screening of the film, Faye is said to have walked out, written Zanuck a stiffly worded note, handed the keys to her dressing room to the studio gate guard and driven off the lot. Despite importuning from Zanuck, she did not appear in another film for seventeen years.

Zanuck's crude excisions undermined not only Alice Faye's character, but the dramatic impetus of the film itself, the character of Emmie Barkley (or June Mills as she is called in the film) ultimately being the more important of the two female leads with her critical redemptive function. But it is the showy bad girls who always get the attention on film and with her looks and attitude Darnell admittedly excels as the bad girl. Also terrific in the film are Anne Revere as intensely man-shy Clara Barkley (Clara Mills in the film), Charles Bickford as the coldly brutal out-of-town police detective Mark Judd, Percy Kilbride of Pa Kettle fame as simpleminded "Pop" and, in a glorified cameo, mellifluous-voiced John Carradine as the spiritualist showman Professor Ernest Madley. Marty Holland's characters are deepened in the film version by this slew of superb performances (even Bruce Cabot, playing Dave Atkins, yet another fervent admirer of Stella, seems less wooden than usual), but it was Holland who provided Preminger and his screenwriter Harry Kleiner with the blueprint.

Generally the beautifully shot film follows the plot of the novel, making much of the setting at Pop's and taking some scenes, like Judd's nasty third degree kid glove beating of suspect Dave Atkins, right from the book (though the even more violent beating of a passing Mexican tramp is omitted from the film). However, in the cinematic version of *Fallen Angel*, Stella's life is extended for about two-thirds of the way through the picture (she dies one-third of the way into the book) and the denouement in which her murderer is revealed is heavily altered, with much of Eric's own investigation getting scrapped in the process. Certainly it is interesting to compare the book with its fine if flawed film adaptation, but Marty Holland's novel stands strongly on its own as an early, much-publicized example of the work of a woman who dared to write her crime "tough," albeit with a certain softer, feminine sheen.

In 1949 the *Los Angeles Daily News* reported that with some of the proceeds from her ample writing career income Marty Holland was building an apartment house in Los Angeles as a business investment. Quipped reporter Darr Smith: "[S]he's one of the few writers in town who puts her money into something besides Scotch whiskey." A niece recollects that Holland, "a tough woman with a big heart," took an interest in the lives of her nieces and nephews and was generous with her money, buying cars for several of her family members. She had been married, her family believed, for a time in the 1930s and was romantically involved in the Forties with crime writer and scriptwriter Steve Fisher (author of *I Wake Up Screaming*), but by the Fifties she was increasingly lonely, had bouts of depression and smoke and drank more than was good for her. (Indeed, recalling Darr Smith's quip, Holland, like other writers, put plenty of her money into

Scotch whiskey—her favorite brand was Four Roses.) Later in life, when she was working on a final novel, *Baby Godiva*, she came down with cancer. Desperately she sought help from faith healer Kathryn Kuhlman but to no avail, passing away in 1971. At her death, Holland had last published fiction two decades earlier, with a pair of novellas, "Terror for Two" (*Scarab Mystery Magazine*, 1951) and "The Sleeping City" (*Thrilling Detective*, 1952). Clearly at that time Marty could still step on the gas, but the tank of her creative machine was running on empty. Happily the criminous legacy of noir's premier mystery woman soon will be taken out in its entirety for yet another thrilling spin.

—December 2022
Germantown, TN

••

Curtis Evans received a PhD in American history in 1998. He is the author of *Masters of the "Humdrum" Mystery: Cecil John Charles Street, Freeman Wills Crofts, Alfred Walter Stewart and British Detective Fiction, 1920-1961* (2012) and most recently the editor of the Edgar nominated *Murder in the Closet: Essays on Queer Clues in Crime Fiction Before Stonewall* (2017) and, with Douglas G. Greene, the Richard Webb and Hugh Wheeler short crime fiction collection, *The Cases of Lieutenant Timothy Trant* (2019). He blogs on vintage crime fiction at *The Passing Tramp*.

Fallen Angel

MARTY HOLLAND

1

It was a big passenger bus making time along the Coast Highway. Outside the windows it was night and you could see fog drifting across the ocean. Inside, it was hot and stuffy: overcrowded. Wartime traveling. Old men smoking cigars, dames eating candy; soldiers, a farmer next to me in the little jump seat in the aisle.

On the other side of me in the seat by the window, a dame of about forty-five was twitching this way and that and giving me sidelong glances. She had a big fanny, a magazine, and gardenia perfume in her hair. Strictly out of boredom, I would have made a couple of faint passes at her and got her really interested, only I couldn't, because I was pretending to be asleep. I was lying back in the seat, my eyes closed, only opening them now and then for a peep at the scenery both inside and out. I half believed my pretended oblivion had me practically sold on the idea that I was really asleep. Which is why I jumped when the driver yelled:

"You can start wakin' up any time now, pal."

I didn't know whether to open my eyes or not. Jesus, but he was getting familiar!

"*You*—" he said, "you with the hat pulled down over your eyes. You can look now. We're stopping in about three minutes to let you off."

"Me?" I said, coming out of it.

He laughed. "Fer-Chris-sake, quit acting."

"Acting?" I echoed. Everybody was looking at me. Especially the squirmy dame.

The driver didn't answer right away. He chewed gum, watching the road with one eye and me in the rearview mirror with the other. He was leaning his elbows on the wheel as he drove. The passengers were all very attentive now—hanging on to his dialogue like he was Saroyan or somebody. On a bus, the driver is always the prima donna. He keeps the spotlight on himself—has a running line of gab from the time he leaves the terminal until he gets off. I'd been listening to him for three hundred miles—and getting an ache you-know-where. He waited until the proper psychological moment, then nailed me with:

"That's an old trick—pretending to be asleep so you can ride farther than your ticket calls for—"

"I—"

"You were awake last stop," he said, "and that was your station. I let you stay on just to see how far you'd carry it."

Everyone laughed.

He was such a wise, dandy guy, this driver!

"I suppose," he went on, enjoying his popularity, "you thought I wouldn't notice you—and you'd get a ride all the way in to Frisco."

I didn't answer.

"Well, mister," he continued, "besides drivin' I got nothin' to do but sit here and count noses in this here mirror."

"And flirt with women that ride in the front seat."

"I wouldn't say that."

"I would."

"I'll talk to you later," he said, "when we stop."

"Fine."

"Of all the chiseling bums," he muttered. "Ever see such a cheap skate as that?"

No one answered.

"Fine," I said. "Just keep on like that."

But he didn't. The back of his neck was red. In a few minutes we stopped. I got off, lugging my two new suitcases after me. I waited. There were a lot of faces at the bus windows, all peering out. The driver got off. He was bigger than me and looked down at me—sort of bored-like: he was thin, angular—had high cheekbones, and I noticed now, calloused knuckles. I saw what was going to happen and didn't wait for it. I let him have it—in the basket. He fell back against the smudgy silver-colored side of the bus—then he came after me. He hit me twice.

When I came to I was sitting on my can on the sidewalk. The bus was gone. There was no one around—just me and the two suitcases, one on either side. I got up; then down again, quick. I waited for my head to stop going round.

In a few minutes the scenery began to clear. I saw the name of

the town:
Walton.

I scooted over to the curb and sat, still groggy. An elderly couple sauntered by with a big shaggy canine on leash. The old dame gave a look my direction. The mongrel lifted one paw and sniffed at me with the air of a pointer. Then they all went on their way—the three of them.

I got to my feet, leaning against a palm tree, and looked down the street. It was like all the California beach towns. Cold and foggy one night—warm and clear as a bell the next. But it was cold and foggy this night—drab and dark and dimmed out. Streetlamps casting pale amber glows through the gray blanket of mist.

The drugstore at the corner was open, and a cocktail bar across the street, a theatre to my right. All the other shops were shut tight—everything quiet. Everything quiet except for the steady pounding of the surf behind me, the squawk of the sea gulls. The salt air was raw and crisp. It smelled good. It smelled especially good after that three hundred miles of stale air on the bus. I thought of the driver again and called him what he was under my breath. It made me feel better.

I felt a gnawing in my stomach. I could visualize thick, juicy beef. I put my hat back on and picked up the suitcases. Hoofing it down the street I saw the sign on a store window: POP'S EATS. In big, black letters.

A bell tingled over the door as I entered. It was warm inside, and there was steam on the windows. I sat up at the counter and waited. No customers, no sign of life. The coffee urn was panting. On the wall, General MacArthur looked down disapprovingly. There was a picture of Roosevelt further up toward the window. F.D.R. was smiling. Above the breakfast cereal rack there was a newspaper photograph tacked to the wall. Roosevelt again, with Churchill—shaking hands.

A small, limp American flag hung over the back partition. Behind that was the kitchen. I heard sound from back there, but still nobody put in an appearance. I tried coughing. It worked.

A time-worn, unshaven gent in shirt sleeves came out through the door and hurried up along the inside of the counter. He set a glass of water before me and wiped his hands on the side of his apron. He was scrawny—like a picked chicken—puffed under the eyes, like his kidneys were out of whack. His nose was long and came to a round delicate pink knob at the end. You could tell this old boy hit the bottle regularly. His hair was gray and thin, shaggy at the sides. I told him my intentions of having steak.

"No meat," he said.

It took a moment for disaster to set in. "Not even a hamburger sandwich?"

His watery eyes focused on me. "No meat." He had a stubborn, belligerent attitude. "I can give you chicken. That's fowl."

"All chicken is foul. I don't want any."

"Young fella—are you aware there's a war goin' on?"

"Yeah. I still don't like chicken."

He glared at me. "How is it a strong fella like you ain't in uniform?"

I felt like fixing him up for false teeth, but I noticed he already had them. "Never mind. Just give me a pack of Luckies—"

He reached under the counter and came up with the cigarettes. I handed him a dollar bill from my wallet. When he came back with the change I'd arranged my identification card so that it fell out on the counter, facing him. It was impressive, this card, gold-edged, with my picture and right thumb print. Up to two days ago, I was an insurance detective, and the card said: Investigator—Federal Bureau of Insurance. I saw that the old geezer's eyes were glued to it, so I jerked it up quick, before he saw too much.

"Golly!" he breathed. "F.B.I.!"

I didn't say anything. I looked at him the way I thought a G-man should look. It had worked the way I'd figured—he'd just get a quick glance—thought the word *Insurance* was *Investigation*. It'll work that way every time. It's only on the second look that you catch on. It'd pulled me out of many a jam. But Grandpa here bit hook, line and sinker.

"Golly! No wonder you ain't in uniform!"

I felt like laughing out loud. But I narrowed my eyes and put on a terrific dead-pan. "You didn't see that card, see? *Remember you didn't see it!*"

He gulped down a breath and thrust back his shoulders. "No siree, I ain't seen it." He regarded me with deep respect. "Reckon I *can* fix you up a steak though," he added slyly, "one I was savin' for m'self. It ain't much of one, but you're welcome to it."

"Make it snappy, mister."

He took my order like a command, and marched into the back. In a minute I heard the sweet sound of a steak sputtering on the grill. He brought out some dishwater soup and a wilted salad which I told him he could put back in the garbage can. But the steak was okay. Nothing that would melt in your mouth, but okay. I cleaned it down to the bone and lapped up some of the weak coffee.

It was about then that she came in.

At first she was just the swish of the door, then I heard her high heels on the cement behind me, and I smelled her perfume. It was perfume like nothing you get for a buck an ounce. It had quality. I heard her voice. It put a chill through me. It wasn't what she said, it was how she said it—husky, low, don't give a damn:

"Well, Pop—is my job still open?"

The old man's head was stuck out of the door in the back. When he saw her his face lit up like Christmas. She called him Pop, but he wasn't her father. You could tell that with one glance.

"*Stella!*" he said hoarsely, and I thought he was going to cry. He came in front of the counter, over to her, his eyes all worship, sick like a St. Bernard. "You can always have your job back here," he told her. His face contorted, as though he were about to approach a touchy subject. "It didn't work out?"

I turned in my seat in the pretense of bending down to get my hat on the next chair. I saw her, my eyes traveling up from the floor. I saw her shoes first. They were small, black patent, with a strap and extreme high heels. Her bare legs were smooth, thin at the ankles, husky at the calves. Her skirt broke at the knees. They were good knees, sleek and tapered. The skirt was tight around her hips and she was all right in that department, too. Her waist was small, and coming up to the breasts she was long.

She was blonde. All frizz. Her hair was short above her ears, fluffed all over her head. She had on a lot of make-up, eyebrows too dark. Blue eyes. I've seen my share of dames but none with eyes like this. Sad. Her lips were brilliant red. Thick lips—you'd say. But that's how I like 'em. She had on a short-sleeved blouse and the strap of her brassiere hung down her arm. I noticed her hand because she held it out. It was bare and white and slender with blood-red polish. I wondered why she was showing Pop her left hand.

"It didn't work out," he said again, but this time it wasn't interrogative.

Her mouth quivered, and then almost savagely she sunk her teeth down into her lower lip. I reached back on the counter, fumbling for my check, but all the time I could see her through the corner of my eye. Pop took her arm and led her to the back of the room, past the partition, out of sight.

"The young fella didn't marry you?" I heard him saying.

"No." There was a muffled sob, then she was crying. I got up and stood by the cash register. I scraped my feet on the cement. Pop came back out.

"That'll be a dollar," he said morosely. "Three cents tax—"

I paid him and picked up my luggage before I got the idea. Damn good suitcases....

I'd bought them in L.A.—fifteen bucks—imitation leather. I got them just a couple of days before the smart boys at the insurance company wised up to the fact that I was drawing down dough, not only from them but from the clients as well: playing both ends against the middle. I figured if I didn't make ends meet on the job it was my own fault. They gypped the customers, I gypped everybody: for a while, that is. Then I got out of town, one jump ahead of the sheriff. And if I hadn't got wound up in a crap game the night before I'd have had enough dough-re-mi for a bus ticket to Frisco. As it was—here I was halfway, or forty odd miles beyond that, and broke. Four bucks in my pocket. But I had this flashy dime store luggage and a tongue in my head that nature put there to use.

Pop here looked like Simple Simon. The longer I looked at him the more simple he seemed. I got the idea he was two notches removed from a moron. Maybe hardening of the arteries was setting in or something. Anyway, he was soft, and soft-hearted. Guys who bum around on one job and the other—from high and low pitch on can openers to insurance cops—have a word for guys like Pop. It's spelled j-e-r-k. If I hadn't already given him the F.B.I. routine, I'd have sold him a subscription to the *Saturday Evening Post* and told him I was working my sister through college. But I had the cases, so I gave him a pitch on them.

"Sure hate to part with this luggage."

Pop was still thinking about Stella, because he didn't hear me at first. I had to repeat it. He perked up a little then and studied the suitcases.

"You say you have to part with 'em?"

I looked regretful. "Yeah—and genuine rawhide suitcases are hard to find. They're not making them anymore. 'Course, what use have I for them? Might as well sell them to somebody—"

"How much you askin'?" He was interested now.

I shrugged. "I'd let them go cheap. Forty apiece, maybe. 'Course I'd be taking a loss. They're brand new. I paid a hundred bucks for the two only a week ago." I looked longingly at the cases. "Don't know if I should let them go so cheap or not."

"Mighty nice grips." Pop was walking around to them. "You can tell they're gen-u-wine all right."

"Yeah. They'd last you a lifetime."

He was thoughtful. "I could use 'em, 'cause I'm takin' a trip—if Stella don't run off no more." He looked up at me. "If you'll take forty apiece, bring 'em back in the mornin'. I got to draw some money from the bank—"

"Sure." I started for the door.

"What's your name, young fella?"

I turned around. "Stanton. Eric Stanton."

"Glad to know you, Mister Stanton." He walked over to me and shook my hand. "I'm Ben Elliot. Everybody calls me Pop."

"You're getting a good bargain on these cases, Pop."

"How come you won't be needin' 'em? Ain't you on a vacation?"

"That's right. Vacation." My voice hardened. "Understand?"

He nodded slowly and his eyes bulged. I knew he was dying to ask me if there was something going on in town that the F.B.I. was called in to investigate.

He said: "You're stayin' here?"

It was hard for me to keep my eyes off the back partition. "For a while," I said.

He nodded knowingly, as if there were some great secret between us.

I left the place and registered at the first hotel. A buck a night. In my room, I hung up my clothes and put my underwear in the dresser drawer. I found a half bottle of whiskey I'd forgotten about. I drank it before I hit the hay. But even there in the dark, listening to the ocean, I kept thinking about this blonde—this Stella.

Jesus!

2

The next morning I waited until around eleven before I hauled the empty suitcases back down to Pop's. He wasn't there, but she was. She didn't have on a waitress uniform. I guess she thought she was too good for that. She wore a little fancy apron over a thin blue dress. I put the cases to one side and slid down at the counter.

There was a young couple a few seats away. I saw they were finishing breakfast, so I stalled, hoping they'd leave soon. Stella set a glass of water before me and a soiled breakfast menu. She acted like she didn't think I was so hot. She went over to the sink and began drying glasses.

After a while I pulled my eyes back to the menu. Instead of calling out my order to her I waited for her to come back over. She did after a few minutes.

She didn't have so much make-up on today and she looked a little tired. Her lipstick was smeared, like she'd just finished eating breakfast herself.

"What'd'ya want?" She said it glumly, with a heave of her chest.

I said: "Two fried eggs, toast and spuds."

She moved down to the end of the counter to see if the couple leaving had left enough dough. I picked up a newspaper and pretended to read. But all the time I was watching her through the corner of my eye. She glanced back at me just once. Then with the eraser on her pencil she rubbed out part of the check on which she had previously written. She marked it over—which was an old trick. She took the dollar bill and the change over to the cash register. I watched her throw the change in the till. A moment later she stooped down. I saw her slip the greenback into her shoe.

She went into the kitchen for what seemed a hell of a long time to fix a couple of eggs. Finally she came out carrying a plate. She set it down before me.

"Coffee?" She didn't look at me, but past me.

I tried to get her eye by smiling, but she was all ice. "Yeah. Cream and sugar." When she set down the cup I said: "Why do you put dollar bills in your shoes?"

I'd meant it to be cute. But the way she coiled up reminded me of a diamondback rattler.

"That was a tip," she said without blinking an eyelash. "And I'll thank you to mind your own business." She looked straight in my eyes. I got a shiver up my back.

I was only kidding her, trying to get a rise out of her, leading up to asking for a date. I had this one figured. I'd doped her all out last night in the hotel room.

"You don't have to get sore," I said. "I really meant to ask you how you'd like to go out with me tonight."

"I wouldn't like it." The comeback was quick.

Blood was hot in my temples, but I held the smile. Pop came in through the front door then. He began peeling off the greenbacks that amounted to eighty bucks. He took the suitcases to the back, acting like a kid with new toys. I heard him snapping and unsnapping the locks from behind the partition.

Stella was looking past me—but she saw me all right. There was something electric between us. I felt it, and I knew she felt it. She felt everything I did.

"Eighty dollars for those cases," she sneered. "It's highway robbery—"

I managed to grin. "No worse than petty thievery. The jail sentence's the same."

Her head jerked up. She went back to drying the glasses. I was wise to her all right. But she was on to me too. She was watching *me* through the corner of her eye.

I tried smiling again. "I can take you any place you want to go."

"I don't go out with strangers," she said. "Especially those who have anything to sell."

I laughed. "I'm no traveling salesman—if that's what you mean. The luggage was my own. I sold it to Pop as a special favor to him."

"I'll bet!"

I lowered my voice. "Why don't you want to go out with me?"

"I guess it's because I don't like you."

I winced. I felt the blood draining from my cheeks. I sat there staring at her. I tried laughing it off, but I was trembling.

Pop, from the back, had evidently been eavesdropping, because he came out now, up behind the counter.

"Stella," he said, "be more respectful to the customers. Mr. Stanton here is an influential man—"

Her laugh sent a chill down my spine. Suddenly her face sobered. She went to the back, behind the partition. I blurted to Pop:

"It's a wonder you have people like that working for you!"

He leaned over the counter and whispered: "She ain't herself. She's had a sad experience—"

"Yeah," I said hotly. "A soldier."

Pop shook his head. "A bus driver."

I was still trembling. "What time does she get off work?"

"Eight."

"All right," I said loud enough for her to hear, "you tell her I'll be waiting outside at eight! I'm going to take her to a movie!"

I slammed the door behind me.

I thought eight o'clock would never come. I walked around town and went up to my room and read. I went down to the hotel coffee shop and had a sandwich and beer. I went back up to my room and read some more. Hours dragged one by one. At seven I shaved and took a shower. I put on all clean clothes and slicked back my hair. A few minutes before eight, I walked slow down to the restaurant. I passed a flower shop and bought a gardenia corsage. Next door from the joint, I waited.

It wasn't two minutes before she came out. She'd evidently gone home and changed clothes in the afternoon because she was dressed up. She was all in black—which ordinarily I don't like. But with that blonde hair it was a knockout. There was a white flower in her hair. And she had on that perfume again. I smelled it six feet away.

She came closer and I noticed that her eyebrows were all pulled out, penciled on, a thin line. Her lips were red and full and soft. She took my arm and I felt my pulse quickening.

"I knew you'd go out with me," I lied.

She shrugged. "Why not? You're taking me to a movie, aren't you?"

"Sure."

"Pop's a nice old fool," she said. "I don't like to see him buy lousy suitcases. Maybe I'm out to protect his interests—or maybe I want to see what makes you tick. What you doing in town?" she asked flippantly. "Casing a bank or something?"

I laughed. "What kind of people do you run around with?"

She looked straight up at me. "Not your kind."

The laugh froze on my face. I was flustered all of a sudden. "Here—" I handed her the florist box.

She tore the ribbon off and sniffed down at the gardenias. "Thanks," she said drily, "but these things give me hay fever. I can't stand them." She smiled and pointed to her hair. "That's why I wear the artificial ones."

I guess I was too excited, just having her near me, to care about anything. I threw the flowers past the curb. "You sure you want to go to a movie?"

"It's all right. Unless you'd rather see a séance."

I stopped walking and looked at her. "A what?"

"Séance," she repeated languidly. "Professor Ernest Madley is at the City Hall."

"Who's he?"

She looked at me as if I weren't quite bright. "He's the world's most famous spiritual medium."

"Then what's he doing in this hick town?"

Her nose tilted upward. "He's only traveling through. Since the war he doesn't go to Europe anymore."

"You sure know a lot about the guy."

"I can read," she said haughtily, "and folders telling about him have been mailed all over town. Besides he was in the restaurant talking to me most all afternoon." A smile played on her lips. "He asked me to come backstage after the meeting tonight."

"Oh, a romance?" I said.

She laughed. "Nothing like that—but I guess he is stuck on me. Funny, isn't it?"

"Yeah—it's a riot." I felt lousy all of a sudden. "You think he actually gets through to the spooks?"

She hesitated, then said: "Oh, I think Professor Madley does."

It was my turn to laugh. "Ever *see* him talk to the dead?"

"Now that's an absurd question. He's never been in town before. But everybody's turning out."

"Sure you want to go there?" I was hoping she didn't.

She thought for a moment. "Might be better than a movie. And he's only going to be in town tonight."

"Okay. Where do we go?"

"City Hall."

"That alone should prove to you he's a fake," I said. "The only mediums I ever heard of commune in a small, dark room. How can the guy work on a stage before an audience?"

"I don't know. But what's the difference. It might be entertaining."

"Yeah," I said, "it might at that."

We turned in at the City Hall.

3

At a table in the lobby I bought tickets. A dollar a throw. Stella and I breezed inside. The house lights were bright, the place small and stuffy, and jammed full. The seating capacity was around a hundred, and several people were standing along the side walls. We edged our way down and stood halfway back from the stage.
The audience was mostly females. Gum-chewing housewives in wash dresses. One or two with kids on their laps. The males that were there looked henpecked, dejected. It was the women who were excited, faces flushed. There was a murmur of tense whispering throughout.
A faded blue curtain ornamented the stage. We stood only a minute before the house lights dimmed, and a purple glow reflected through the curtains. The audience was hushed expectancy. Finally from the middle of the curtains a man stepped out and held up his hands for quiet.
He was a tall, thin, anemic, with deep-sunken eyes. He looked as though he carried the burdens of the world on his shoulders. He looked like a spook. He made a speech asking for co-operation throughout Professor Madley's appearance. He said that Madley's mother was the Princess Algeb Madley, the famous occult of India; that she'd died years ago. Hence she was Madley's spiritual guide. I gathered that that meant the old lady rounded up the spirits for Madley to talk to. His voice was strictly zombie. When he finished I resisted the urge of giving him a healthy Bronx cheer. How anybody could believe that hocus-pocus was in itself a phenomenon. But this doltish audience was all impressed.
The curtains opened. The stage was bare except for a table in the rear, covered with a black gold-edged cloth. Lamps from offstage threw on this a purple glow.
Then Madley came out. He was pudgy in a tuxedo. He was red-faced and bald. He said that he must have absolute quiet, that with such a large audience it was difficult for them to come through. *Them* meant the spooks, no doubt. His voice was high-pitched and hesitant: reminiscent of a fight referee. If he'd been

smart he'd made his zombie assistant the medium. That one looked the part. This one looked like a beer guzzler. He wasn't convincing. I'll give him credit for only one thing: he had nerve!

He went back to the table and sat down. His eyes closed, and then he began to mumble indistinguishably. "Madre," I heard him say once, which everybody knows is Spanish for mother. I wondered how the Princess' spirit understood it, being she was Indian herself. He gave out with a few words of Greek—then Latin. The guy missed his calling, I thought. He should have been a foreign ambassador somewhere.

He sat there dogo for several minutes. Then he rose. With arms outstretched he walked slowly upstage. He stood there with his eyes closed, beer oozing out of his pores. I guess he was supposed to be in a trance by now and he's succeeded in communing with his old lady, because he said:

"The spirit of Henry Weilder has come through. He wishes word with Mary Weilder, or friends or relatives—"

The audience gasped. A plump woman in a big flowered dress, not three feet away from me, knocked the kid off her lap and bolted to her feet.

"Here—" she blurted. "I'm Mary Weilder." She kept sucking in her breath.

Necks craned. People slid around in their seats. Heads went back and forth, from Madley to this Mary Weilder. When all was quiet again the great man spoke:

"Henry asks you to take better care of your health and not to worry so much about the children. That is all."

"I will," the woman stammered, "you tell him I will—"

She kept standing there until Madley called:

"Josephine Potter desires word with Conrad Potter, or friends or relatives—"

There was a murmur of voices. A man in the first row stood up. I could only see the back of his head, but his voice was quick and jerky. "I'm Josephine's brother."

Madley nodded. He kept his eyes closed. Once or twice he tapped his forehead with his fingers. "Josephine asks me to tell you that she is very happy where she is. To tell Conrad that she is happy, and asks him not to grieve. She asks you to tell him that she has made many wonderful friends—and everything is beautiful and kind where she is—"

"I—I'll see him tonight," the man said. "I'll tell Conrad."

It went on like that for an hour. Madley giving out messages equally vague and simple. And I was getting bored. Bored and disgusted and sore. Madley was fake. I began counting over the heads in the audience. A dollar a seat. It gave me a sinking feeling. He was cleaning up. And I'd been gypping, chiseling here and there, trying to pick up a buck. The guy was smart after all. Smart or dumb he was making a fortune. A hundred and twenty bucks tonight! That was dough! Furthermore he had everybody's respect. Everybody was ogle-eyed, including Stella. She watched him like a schoolgirl watches Sinatra.

"Let's scram out of here," I said.

She gave me a quick, impatient look. "Not yet." Her eyes were for Madley again.

He called out another name. A girl in the back stood up.

"*I'm* Emmie Barkley," she said hoarsely.

Madley was silent for several seconds, then he said: "Your father wants to know if there's anything you wish to ask him."

A good, routine question, I thought.

"Why, why," the girl stammered, "I—no—" She caught her breath. "Yes—yes I *could* ask him something. About the money. Ask him, please, if I should invest it the way I've planned—"

Madley looked stumped. Finally he replied: "No, your father asks you to find a safer investment. War bonds possibly—but not to make any risky investments."

"All right," the girl said. "Tell him I'll do as he says—"

Stella edged over to me. "Her father died a few months ago," she whispered, "and left her ten thousand dollars."

"Ten thousand?" I echoed. Those were nice round figures. "How do you know that?"

"I read it in the paper," Stella said. "There are two Barkley sisters. Their father left them ten thousand each."

I watched this Emmie Barkley as she sank down in the chair. She was wearing a sweater and skirt, no hat. Her hair was dark brown, shiny, parted in the middle, fastened with a barrette at the nape of her neck. Her face was small and oval, with a clean, healthy look.

I was still eying her when the séance ended abruptly. The lights came on, and the gullible began to file out. Everybody was talking excitedly.

Back outside, Stella said: "He's awfully good, isn't he?"

"He's a phony!" I said.

"Why, I don't know how you can say that. After all he did tonight."

I had to laugh. "Listen—all he did was go to the morgue and look through the files. He got the names of all the obituaries and living relatives. Naturally most everybody with dead relatives would come to the meeting. And the messages he made up himself."

She looked at me sullenly. "I wish you hadn't told me that. It takes the thrill out of it."

"Don't you want to know the truth?"

"Not always," she replied. Then: "I'm thirsty."

We went into the first cocktail bar.

At a table with beers before us, I still thought about this fake medium. I didn't know so many people believed in the stuff. But I guess you only need records to go by. I remembered reading somewhere that in New York alone, $25,000,000 is spent annually on that kind of hokum. I thought about Emmie Barkley and the ten grand. It all kept milling around in my head.

Stella and I sat there drinking beers and listening to the juke box. It got later.

"You live alone?" I asked her.

"No. A rooming house."

"That's okay. Let's go over there."

She gave me a look. "No visitors are allowed after ten."

I asked her if she didn't want a couple of whiskeys. She didn't. I asked her if she'd like to go for a walk. She thought for a moment and said well, all right. We got up and went outside and started walking.

We turned on a side street and went down to the ocean. I suggested walking on the beach. We walked on the wet sand where the tide had gone out. The tide was way out, but in the distance you could see the frothy tops of the waves, like soap suds all over the water. There was a cold breeze, and the moonlight was bright. We sat down by a cluster of palm trees.

She folded her arms over her bare legs and looked out at the ocean. Her hair was yellow in the night. Somehow she reminded me of a big, chubby doll.

"I'd like to get on a boat," she said, "and sail way out there."

"Where to?"

"Anywhere. Anywhere to get away from this hickville. I hate this town."

"Been here long?"

"Six months. My home's in Arizona. That's where Mom is."

"You can always sail back home," I said.

She shook her head. "I burned my bridges when I left."

"Have a falling out with your folks?"

She drew a design in the sand with her finger while she talked. "No. I haven't got folks—the way you really think of them. My dad died when I was just a baby."

"Oh."

"Everything was okay," she went on, "until Mom took in a boarder."

"That was bad?"

"Not at first," she replied huskily. "It got bad when he started getting ideas."

"He did?"

She looked up and nodded. "Finally I bounced a flower pot over his head. I got out and never went back. I don't know—I might've killed him."

I changed the subject quick, told her all about myself, how I'd been kicked around since I was a kid—bumming here and there. I went into a long-winded dissertation on my old man, how he never worked a lick in his life, how my mother worked in a department store for sixteen bucks a week and kept up the house on it.

I said: "The most vivid thing I can remember was that worn-out razor strap hanging in the bathroom—and my old man never used it to sharpen a razor. Hell, he kept the heat on me so bad I had to leave home when I was thirteen."

I told her how I rode the rails through ten states and wound up in San Diego, California. I got a job washing dishes for a couple of months, then went on into Mexico.

"When you were only thirteen?" she said.

"Yeah. But I looked older. I was tall. I was skinny, though—because I was sick so much when I was a kid."

I even told her about the time I didn't eat for two days, how I sold shoelaces from door to door. By the time I finished I had her feeling sorry for me.

"You've had it even worse than I have," she said.

"Yeah." I wondered what to say next. I saw she had a wristwatch on. It had sparkling stones all around it.

"Nice watch."

"Those diamonds are real," she said.

"Present from somebody?"

"Huh-uh. I bought it myself."

I decided enough time had wasted. I pulled her over close. She squirmed, ready to fight, and I let her go.

"You've got a nerve!" She bounced to her feet. "Keep your hands off!"

I got up. I grabbed her again and held her—so tight this time she couldn't budge an inch. I crushed my mouth down on hers. After a moment her lips parted, and everything was quiet. There was just the murmur of the ocean and the wind rattling the palms.

4

It wasn't until a week later that the plan jelled in my mind. I'd thought about it ever since the séance, studying the possibilities. I was sure it would work, yet I needed a sounding board. I decided to tell Stella the first thing.

At a quarter to eight, I beat it down from the hotel to the restaurant. Out in front, a funny tingling hit the pit of my stomach. The joint was all dark, the front door locked. The streetlamp in front reflected through the window. I opened the screen door and cupped my hands on the sides of my eyes and peered in.

Suddenly the door opened. It startled me. Stella stood there, her eyes starry in the darkness. She had on her hat and coat.

"I wondered if you were going to show up," she said lazily. "I was going on home."

"Pop gone?"

She nodded. "He always leaves me to close up."

I slid in through the door, snapped the latch so nobody else could get in. I stood beside her, looking down at her. I was panting like a dog. "There's something I have to talk to you about—"

"What is it?" Her face was very sober.

"Sit down at the counter with me—"

We sat there with the streetlamp shining down on our faces. Outside fog rolled past the windows. From across the street I heard the faint music of a juke box. I said:

"Remember Emmie Barkley—the dame at the séance—the one with the ten thousand bucks?"

"What about her?"

"Remember she asked the medium about investing the money?"

Stella nodded vaguely.

"And remember how we've been talking for a week now about clearing out? We were saying if we had the *dough*—" I was so excited over what I had to tell her I could scarcely get my breath.

"What you driving at?"

I grinned. "I'm not such a bad-looking guy, am I? I know my way around, don't I?" I chucked her under the chin. "You got to admit I have you going—"

"You don't love yourself much!"

I laughed.

"You look all right," she said, "to people who don't know you. It's your insides that are rotten, Eric." She looked straight up at me. "I'm dumb, but I know what people are. I know that much. I knew what you were the first night I saw you in here."

My hand toyed with the sugar bowl. "Don't make me sore," I said. "No dame that knocks down dollar bills should be criticizing other people. Let's stop this petty bickering. We both know each other for what we are." I took her hand. "We're alike, Stella. We're the same people. You got to admit it—"

She sighed, and her chest went up. "So what are you getting at?"

I took a deep breath and lowered my voice. "I got a plan where I can clean up and we can both get the hell out."

Her eyes widened. "My God—don't tell me you're going to rob somebody!"

"Me? Do I look like a sucker?" I said drily. "My plan involves Emmie Barkley. It's painless extraction. Nobody gets hurt. Get it?"

She studied me through the darkness. Finally she said: "I read in the newspaper about Emmie getting the money. I never saw her except that once at the séance. But something tells me she's too smart for a phony like you—"

"Don't call me names. I think you're jealous 'cause I'm going to make a play for her. I'm going to give her the romance of her life!"

"So that's it." Her nose went up. "You ought to be ashamed of yourself."

"Shut up," I said softly. "You want to blow out of here—isn't that what you've been squawking about! You want me to say, 'I love you, Stella,' and put a ring on your finger—"

Her eyebrows narrowed. "Listen—you think *all* I want is to get married? Let me tell you something—I know a guy who's dying to marry me. He's got plenty of money; he said he'd buy me anything I wanted."

"Who is this guy?"

"Never mind. I'm only telling you about him to show you I

wouldn't marry just anybody. I wouldn't marry him if he had five million. Honest, I wouldn't, not even if he had five million. Don't you see—I got to be in love."

I squeezed her hand. "You lie low, baby, while I take this broad over and you'll get me all wrapped up in cellophane."

She stared at me and didn't say anything.

"It may take a month," I went on. "It may take two months. I'll sneak in to see you all along. We can't be seen together. You know how it is in a small town—the long hairs'll start gossiping. Emmie'd find out. It'd ruin everything."

"Emmie Barkley wouldn't be seen with you—"

I smiled. "I think she will. She may even want my advice." I got off the chair and stood beside her. I closed my eyes and began tapping my forehead. "They're coming through—" I said in a zombie voice.

"You're going to pass yourself off as a *spiritual medium?*"

"If that's the only way I can get acquainted with her, I will."

"Nobody'd believe it."

"They'll believe it, all right. I could rent me some kind of a place, fix up some purple lights. Maybe even send into L.A. for a trumpet. That Madley guy's a ham!"

She bristled. "He's a real gentleman! And let me tell you something else—he studied for years and years to get where he is. If you think—"

"He's still a ham!" I said. "I'll not only advise Emmie Barkley how to invest her money, but I'll personally invest it for her."

"My God, you're serious!"

"I could pass myself off as anything. Nobody in town knows me yet."

"Except Pop. He'd give you away."

I shook my head. "I'll have a talk with Pop. Hell, he thinks I'm one of Hoover's G-men, looking for certain people. He thinks I'm staying here incognito. I could tell him the spiritual setup is a phony, but I had to have some excuse for staying in town without arousing suspicions as to who I really am. He'll believe it."

"You're sure of yourself. I wouldn't be surprised if Emmie saw through you right away."

"Don't be like that," I told her. "If ever a dame had me going, you have, Stella. You're everything I ever wanted. But you need a decent break. We both need a decent break. With dough like that we can go away—keep moving. See everything there is to see. But where in the hell would we wind up broke? We'd be living in a broken-down house somewhere, like ordinary people. And that's no fun." I put my arm around her. "But we don't need words. We never did need words. No matter where we'd been on this earth, we'd been drawn together. With some people it's like that."

Her face was radiant. "You do love me, don't you?"

"Sure." I put my hand on her bare knee. "Let's go for a walk."

A light faded from her eyes. Her voice was hard suddenly. "No, it's too damp out."

I thought quick. "Did Pop leave the griddle fire on?" I pointed to the back partition. "I can hear something simmering back there—"

"I better go look," she said. "Once I've snapped the night lock from the outside, I can't get back in. Pop never did give me a key."

When I left her that night we'd agreed on not being seen together anymore at all.

5

The church was small and white, with climbing rose bushes on either side of the door. The lawn was green and freshly mowed. I heard the organ from inside, the whole congregation singing. I didn't know the name of the hymn but I'd heard it before. I'd heard my old man sing it in church while he kicked my shins to keep me singing it too. I was quite young, but I didn't like the song. I didn't like organs.

I went inside and stood in the last row. Nobody paid any attention to me. They kept right on singing. Over their heads I glimpsed the preacher, standing before the pulpit. Singing too. The music stopped abruptly and everybody sat down. My eyes began searching the backs and sides of heads for Emmie Barkley.

I wasn't sure I'd find her here. But chances were she attended the early Sunday morning service. I knew which church she went to because I happened to catch her name in the gossip column of the town newspaper. It gave several names of people who'd participated in last Sunday evening's pageant of *Ruth and Naomi*. Among them was Miss Emmeline Barkley. So I decided it might be wise to start pitching right away. I hadn't heard any word from the outfit I'd written to—to find out how much those trumpets cost. Besides, I was getting cold feet on that deal. I was all hopped up about it when I told Stella. But later I thought it over and got cold feet. I couldn't be sure that Emmie'd come to my spiritual meetings. Why should she, when Madley'd already given her advice. I decided not to get involved with the long hairs of this burg. The thing for me to do was to get this Emmie alone. Then I could give her all the chicanery I wanted. I could feed her a line a mile long.

So I kept combing the room for her. And the preacher began the sermon. He started out in a low, quiet voice. The subject matter was minus. He raved on and on about nothing, making it sound like something. He made a play on the word "sinner." Upon each repetition his voice struck more reverent pathos.

I thought he was good for two hours. But he stopped finally and the collection baskets were passed. I dropped in a slug. After that was over they all stood again and sang, *Jesus Loves Me*. I sang along with them, keeping an eye out for Emmie.

Suddenly I noticed there was a girl on the platform playing the organ: Emmie. Her back was toward me, but I recognized the hair—tied back in a barrette at the nape of her neck.

The song ended, and people filed out the one middle aisle. I stayed in my seat, waiting, wondering exactly how I was going to strike up with her.

The last of the congregation straggled out. Then I saw her, still at the organ. The flap on the bench was open and she was putting away the hymnbooks. I waited till the preacher walked into the back room, then I got up and moved down to her.

I noticed her hair was nice. Clean and brown and shiny, with a faint suggestion of curl. She wore a yellow jersey dress with a bronze pin on her shoulder. Her figure wasn't bad—even in the dress. Slim hips, wide shoulders, and very full-breasted. She used make-up too sparingly—just a touch of rouge on her lips. Her eyebrows were kind of thick, but they looked good on her that way. In a close up, her eyes were light brown with a virginal gleam. She wasn't bad at all. But still you couldn't escape facts: she was an old maid at twenty-five.

When she looked up and saw me standing there watching her she gasped. Then she was all apology:

"I'm so sorry. I thought everyone had gone—and you frightened me."

She had a nice, clear voice. But it was Snow White around the edges. I knew I had to use the soft pedal. I said:

"I wanted to tell you I liked your music."

Her cheeks flushed. "Why, that's just awfully nice of you to say so." She crumpled a handkerchief in her hand. "Do you play yourself?"

"No, I—" I groped for words. "The organ is my—well, I like it."

She wet her lips. "Your first time here?"

"Yeah."

Her eyes searched my coat lapels. "You didn't get a ribbon?"

I shook my head. "Should I have?"

"All first-timers get ribbons."

"That's okay. I won't miss it."

"It isn't all right at all." She hurried up the short flight of steps, up to the pulpit. "I'll find you one—"

"Never mind," I called. "I don't need it."

"But you must have a ribbon."

Emmie flitted all over the place looking here and there, in drawers, cupboards. Finally she retreated. Back down the steps, she said:

"I'm so sorry. I just can't find one."

I put on a smile. "Thanks, anyway."

There was a silence while I tried to think of something to say, and she came in with:

"Are you staying in town long, Mr.—"

"Stanton. Eric Stanton."

She shook my hand. "I'm very pleased to know you, Mr. Stanton. My name is Emmie Barkley. Since you're new—I know you'll want to know the best church. I'm sure you'll find this one better than the others. It's—" She was looking up into my eyes. I don't know what she saw but she broke off suddenly. Her gaze went to the floor. "Oh—yes, as I was saying, I prefer this church. Please understand that I'm not saying anything against the other churches. It's just that I, personally, prefer this one—"

"Sure, sure."

"I knew you'd want to know the best place of worship."

"Yeah. It's a pretty small town from where I'm used to. What do you do when you're lonely?"

Her eyes were still on the floor. They came up slowly, guiltily. "Lonely?" she echoed. She gave a short laugh. "I can't help you there. I have no remedy for that."

"Then you're never lonely?"

"Oh, yes—" She was avoiding my eyes again. "—of course. Everyone must be lonely at times."

"I'm lonely all the time."

Her face colored. "You're coming back tonight?" she asked awkwardly. "You really should. It's going to be a fine sermon. The Reverend Thomas is speaking on Hitler and the Devil. It starts at eight o'clock."

I gestured to the organ. "You playing this thing tonight?"

"No. Reverend Thomas' wife plays on Sunday evenings. She sings, too. Contralto. You really should hear her, she's—"

"I'll come back tonight if you'll sit through the preaching with me." (I'm going too fast, I thought, but it was too late—I was already in high gear.)

"Well, I—" She gulped down a breath. "I—"

A feminine voice from outside suddenly boomed:

"*Emmie—*"

"My sister," Emmie said breathlessly. "She's been waiting for me outside in the car—all this time." She turned to the door. "Just a minute, Clara—"

Clara came in then, marching truculently. She was a tall gal in her thirties. She had straight brown hair, done piously in a knot. A small, brimmed hat sat on the top of her head. She was flat-busted in a brown crepe dress. She held one hand to the side of her head, as if it hurt.

"What's keeping you?" she hurled at Emmie. "Have you no regard for my headache!"

"Oh, Clara, dear—I want you to know Mr. Stanton. He's a first-timer." Emmie smiled up at me. "This is my sister—Mrs. Reeder."

"How do you do." Clara surveyed me coldly, then looked back to Emmie. "If you're not in the car in two minutes, you'll walk—"

Emmie was flustered. "I'll be right out, dear—"

Clara turned and walked out.

"Well—good-bye—" Emmie took a few steps to the door. When I didn't say anything she turned back to me. "I—I've never sat through a sermon with a first-timer before—but I'm on the welcoming committee. So I'm sure it'll be all right. That is—if Clara has her headache tonight and doesn't come back with me. She doesn't approve of—" She broke off. "She's—"

"I'll meet you out in front of the church at eight."

"All right," she said, relieved. "Eight o'clock." She turned and hurried outside.

I heard the car driving off. Then I left the church.

I couldn't help smiling.

Eight o'clock came and no Emmie. I watched the cars drive up and saw everybody go in to the church. The doors were closed finally and singing began inside. I stood on the sidewalk wondering what Stella was doing. Locking the joint up about now, I supposed.

Suddenly an automobile came whizzing down the street. Emmie sat behind the wheel. She didn't see me. She pulled over to the curb. I crossed the street and caught her before she had a chance to get out.

"You're late," I said good-humoredly.

Her face lit up and she smiled. "I thought I wouldn't be able to make it. Clara's headache was better at the last minute. I had to dissuade her on coming along—"

"She wouldn't have let you sit with me?"

"She'd have tried to prevent it. But please don't feel badly. Clara doesn't approve of anyone." She smiled again. "I don't mean to sound unkind. She's really a dear, but she—" She glanced at the church. "We must hurry inside now."

I had to work fast.

"We're late already," I said. "What do you say we skip church?" Without waiting for her answer I went around to the other side of the car. When I got in the seat beside her she was still hesitating. But you could tell she didn't want to hear that sermon any more than I did. She looked as if she might be thinking: To hell with Hitler and the Devil! This may be the romance I'm looking for!

Her eyes shone. "I hate to miss that sermon."

"Same here. But how can I talk to you when the preacher's talking?"

She caught her breath. "Where do you suggest going?"

"We can always drive along the beach."

She started the motor without further ado. She didn't waste time. We were off. It was a '37 Plymouth, Tudor sedan. Gun-metal gray and the side windows were cracked from wear. There was a plaid blanket thrown over the front seat. To keep the upholstery clean.

Driving along the beach highway, I smelled smoke. It curled up from the floor board. I told Emmie her feed line was off. She said she'd been going to turn the car in for a newer model, but prices were so high she'd decided to keep it until after the war.

After a while she asked: "What kind of a car do you drive?"

"Cadillac. '41. I sold it before I left L.A." I pointed to a clearing off the road. "Let's pull over there. We can talk better if you're not driving."

She turned off the highway and pulled up the brake. We were facing the ocean now. The night was dark, the horizon barely visible. Below, waves crashed against the rocks.

She sat tense, behind the wheel. I started off with the blarney right away:

"You're the prettiest girl I've seen in town."

She smiled.

"And you don't bother with a lot of paint on your face."

"I hate artificiality."

I agreed with her. Then I said: "Now what's all this about your sister?" Something told me that this Clara babe was going to be bad business. She might louse everything up. I thought I'd better find out everything I could about her, so I'd know how to handle her.

Emmie's eyes clouded. "I don't like to talk about it. But Clara feels that she doesn't have much to live for—since her husband went away—"

"He went away? Where to?"

"Nobody knows. He just up and left Clara two years ago—in the middle of the night."

Visualizing Clara, I didn't blame him much. I said: "That right?"

She nodded. "Clara's just content to live with the memory of Sam Reeder. Consequently, she thinks about herself so much she has violent headaches all the time. It's because she has nothing to occupy her mind. She thinks all men are terrible beasts. She's trying to make my life as empty as her own. She criticizes everyone I bring home—right in front of them."

"Why don't you move some place else?"

"I've been going to—several times. Then Clara starts crying—carrying on. I always feel sorry for her and I stay—"

"That's too bad. Because I'd like to start calling on you at your house."

She was wistful. "I wouldn't try it if I were you. It'd be just like the rest. Clara talks to them—and they never come back."

"I'd come back. She couldn't faze me."

Emmie smiled softly. "Yes, she could. She'd start accusing you of going out with me for my money. That's what she told the last young man that came calling."

A chill went up my spine. "That's ridiculous! Do you have money?"

"An inheritance my father left me," she said simply.

I didn't say anything. I sat there thinking. After a while she said: "Your name is Eric. That's a nice name. It was my grandfather's—on my mother's side."

"You and Clara live with your mother?"

"No. My mother died when we were very young. Clara's always had to look after me. You see, I'm five years younger than she—and she still looks after me. She forgets that I'm not a little girl anymore." She paused. "Good heavens—I shudder when I think how old I am."

"All of twenty-five," I said.

She was nervous again. "I'm thirty. In four months I'll be thirty-one. And I've never been married." Her eyes came up. "How old are you?"

"Twenty-eight."

"Well," she said flustered, "I don't feel thirty. My girl friends are all younger than I—and I like what kids like. I like a circus, you know—things like that. There's a circus in Glenwood. I'm dying to see it. So you see, I'm not old at all, am I? You said I looked twenty-five. Well, I feel younger than that even."

"Sure, sure," I said. "You're only as old as you feel." I thought for a moment. "I feel young myself. I like a circus, too. What'd you say we both go to the circus?"

"Why—that would be nice. Glenwood's only twenty miles. We could drive there Saturday evening maybe."

"It's a date."

There was another silence, then she inquired:

"What kind of work do you do, Eric?"

"I'm sort of a spiritual medium—" I watched her eyes widen.

"Well, good heavens—I'd taken you for anything but that!"

"It's been my life work. I help people with problems more than anything else. *They* come through and tell me how to advise people."

"That's awfully interesting. I was to a séance last week." She paused. "Maybe you know Professor Madley."

"The name sounds familiar."

"I spoke to my father through him. He told me not to invest the money the way I'd planned. But you know something—I had a feeling he didn't talk to my father at all! I'm not saying that he wasn't honest and sincere—but do you *really* speak to the dead? I mean—can you hear their voices and all?"

"Very definitely." My voice was grim. "I've talked to many people of the other world."

"I'm sorry if I've hurt your feelings—but I just wondered about it, that's all. I believe it then, Eric, if you say you have talked to the dead."

"Hundreds of times."

"Then I certainly will follow the advice Professor Madley gave me. In fact, I already have; I've put my money in war bonds."

"You have—already?" I felt a catch in my throat.

"Yes. It's the safest investment I know."

"I've made a lot of money on stocks," I said. "I could make you some good money in stocks."

She shook her head. "I wouldn't put a penny in stocks. My father lost money that way." She paused in thought. "No, I'm going to keep it in war bonds. And I won't cash them in. That is, unless I get married or something." She smiled. "I've always wanted a home of my own. And if my husband can't afford to buy it, well, I'll buy it."

She had a determined air about her, this Emmie. She was a hard nut to crack. I was stuck unless I could get her to cash in those war bonds. I had plenty of thinking to do.

We sat there, listening to the ocean, talking about this and that. Pretty soon she said church must be out. She'd better be getting back. I told her she could drop me off at the hotel. She started the motor again, and drove back down the highway.

We hit the edge of town and then the streetlamps stared dismally. We passed Pop's Place and it was dark inside. I wondered about Stella again. Suddenly the Plymouth creaked to a stop in front of the hotel. It stood shivering with the motor on.

"And Saturday," she said, "we'll go to the circus."

"Sure. Great."

"I'll meet you right here in front—"

"Swell."

"About six o'clock, Eric?"

"Yeah. You be a good girl in the meantime."

She looked up at me like she wanted to be kissed. I wasn't in the mood. I got out of the car and closed the door. We said good night and she looked a little disappointed as she drove away.

I walked slowly upstairs, wondering what I was going to do with this Emmie, wondering how I'd get my hands on that ten thousand bucks.

6

I didn't wonder long. The next morning my mind was made up. I hurried in to see Stella, to see how she was going to take it. I sat up at the counter and pretended to look the menu over, but I was watching Stella. I was never so glad to see anybody in my life. There was something about her that got me. She wasn't all over you. She had that cool aloofness—luscious figure, soft skin. I watched her fill two bowls of cereal.

Suddenly somebody said: "Hey, baby—come here!"

I hadn't noticed the guy. He was sitting up front. I took him in fast. He was immaculate in a black pin-striped suit. White silk shirt and a red tie, a red carnation in the coat lapel. Red sparkling cuff links. His hair was black and straight back. He was sort of flabby all over. He was fortyish, but he was handsome. A little too pretty. His fingernails shone, and he wore a ring on his little finger. I noticed his shoes. They had lifts on the heels.

"Another cup of coffee," he told Stella.

She set the cup down and when he reached for it his coat opened a little. I caught a glimpse of steel. He was no citizen of Walton. I saw him looking Stella over, smiling, breathing her in. I saw Stella smile back at him. She didn't smile actually; there was a play on her lips, and in her eyes. I knew the look all right. I saw red.

The couple sitting next to me got up and left. But this handsome walrus stayed. He stayed and kept glancing at me, waiting for me to leave so he could mix with Stella.

I yelled my order to her. She stopped mooning over the guy long enough to give me some orange juice and a cup of coffee. Handsome glanced at his watch, then got up. Stella went over and took his money. He left a dollar tip on the counter. He looked at her again. He looked at every department. I watched him go outside and get in a black Buick parked across the street.

I saw myself in the mirror. I was pale. I turned to her. "Who's the ugly mug?"

She shrugged. "He came in yesterday for lunch. Been coming

back for meals ever since."

"Yeah? And what else?" I was trembling again. "You been out with him?"

"Of course not. So what if I did?"

"That's a fine attitude! Here I am figuring ways for us to be together and you're treating me like dirt!"

"Don't be so suspicious then."

"You haven't got your eyes on that guy?"

"Don't make me laugh."

I took a deep breath. I felt better. "He had me scared," I said. "The way he kept looking at you, you'd think he knew you."

"He'd like to know me, that's all. He'd like to know me."

"You going to date him?"

"He hasn't even asked me."

I clenched my fist hard. "You didn't answer my question, so I'll answer it for you. You're not going out with that jerk, understand? You do and I'll break every bone in his head!"

A smile flickered across her face. "Now who's jealous! I don't like him; I wouldn't go out with him. Even if he asked me."

I took her hand. I'd never known anyone like Stella before. I was looking up at her like a sick cow. "There's something come up," I said. "I've got to talk to you."

She leaned across the counter and whispered: "Keep it low. Pop's resting on the cot in the kitchen."

I went up to the front of the counter and sat down again. Stella came up.

"It's Emmie," I said quietly. "I'm going to have to marry her."

I saw the reaction it had on her ... I saw her bristling. "Do you think *I* like it?" I was miserable. "Do you think *I* want to be away from you for one minute! You think we can clean up ten grand without having to suffer a little! We got to be sensible!"

I explained to her then how Emmie had all the dough in war bonds, and she wouldn't cash them for any other reason than to buy a house.

"I wasn't so good on the medium business," I said. "Hell, I don't know much about that stuff. Besides, Madley wrecked everything there. He already gave her a message from her old man."

Stella kept looking at me.

"Don't you see," I went on, "I've got to get her to cash in the bonds. I'll get the dough and we'll scram—"

She sighed with a heave of her chest. "Then you and me can never get married, Eric."

"Maybe we'll only take half her dough," I said. "I'll have a legal right to half. I'll get a divorce all right."

She thought for a moment. "I guess it's all right. If that's the only way."

"It's the only way. I've studied every angle and—"

"Emmie's said she'll marry you—in just one night?"

I shook my head. "I haven't even asked her yet—but she'll marry me. She's thirty years old, Stella. She isn't a kid like you. Besides, she's dying to get away from her sister."

"Everybody's dying to get away from something or other," she said glumly. "Go ahead. Marry her."

"In a month we'll be able to clear out. Hell, not even that long. A couple weeks maybe."

A customer came in. I gulped down the rest of my coffee and went out.

7

I sat on an old brown mare, and the merry-go-round went round. Music pounding out the same jerky, monotonous tune. Emmie was on a white steed. She sat across from me, her horse high while mine was low, and vice versa.

It was a picture for sore eyes! It was a picture you'd never forget! She was all in pink, with some kind of glass clips at her neck. And her hair was loose all around her shoulders. She held onto the reins with one hand, the other grasped her purse and the sack of popcorn I'd bought her. All the while she was laughing and talking.

This was her idea of a big night: this was her night to howl! We rode the merry-go-round five times. We waded through sawdust to feed peanuts to the caged monkeys. We saw the fat lady and the thin man, watched a trained bear roller skate. We took in the flea circus and the headless man. We went on the chute-the-chutes and the barrel of fun. I spent four bucks on that kind of damn-foolery!

At nine o'clock we'd seen about everything. We sat on a bench in the sawdust, listening to the echo of the merry-go-round. Emmie watched the colored lights and the silver stars painted on the ceiling of the big tent. I watched a little brunette nautch dancer, about fifty feet away, giving out with a sample of the show. I thought about her all the way home.

Emmie and I were a twosome after that. She always picked me up in front of the hotel, and off we'd go in the Plymouth. Sometimes we parked along the ocean in the car and talked—like we did that first night. Once we went back to Glenville and took in a movie she wanted to see.

One afternoon we drove a couple miles out of town to Cove Beach. Emmie brought lemonade and little sandwiches and we ate lunch on the sand. We swam in the ocean and lay around in the sun. I was beginning to feel like a boy scout!

A couple nights later, she drove me forty miles to a mission town. San Pueblo, or something like that. She dragged me all through the mission, showing me this and that. She said it was hundreds of years old.

That night cost me a buck and a half for our dinners. We ate at a Spanish Café—enchiladas and tacos and frijoles and rice. There was a dance floor in the back of the joint, a juke box playing. Emmie said she wanted to dance, so I walked her around on the floor. I never have been any good at it; I was clumsy as hell. But she said she loved to dance with me.

I remember I drove home that night, and we stopped again along the beach, just before we got into Walton. We were on the ledge overlooking the ocean. The moon was out full and there were a lot of stars in the sky. We sat there not saying anything. A train whistle echoed in the distance and when it died down, she said:

"We've had an awful lot of fun together—"

"Yeah. We sure have." I rested one arm on the seat in back of her. She took it for a romantic gesture. She snuggled over closer.

"I guess we like the same things."

"Yeah."

"I've never had so much fun with anybody before."

"Me either."

"The fellows in this town aren't like you. They're not a bit worldly or sophisticated." She paused. "Eric—"

"Yeah."

"I want to ask you something—something I've never asked a man before..."

"What is it?"

"Will you please—kiss me?"

I looked down at her. She was all sweet sadness. My arm dropped around her shoulder. I grabbed her with the other. I drew her close. Silently and leisurely I bent down and kissed her. I could feel heat radiating all through her. When I released her she had a hard time getting her breath.

"Please—don't think I'm—fast. It's just that you've never kissed me, and I've wanted you to so—awfully much."

"So what's wrong with that? Always do what you want to. Never let anybody push you around." I was getting in a plug against sister Clara. "Nobody can live your life for you. When two people like us meet and click, it might be the real thing."

"Isn't it the truth?"

I remembered something I'd heard Charles Boyer or somebody say on the screen. It was unadulterated corn, but I said it:

"Fate has brought us together, Emmie."

She nodded, her eyes moist. "Isn't it crazy how we can tell right away?" She laughed in her throat. "We know so little about each other—yet we *know!*"

"I want to marry you. Now that I've found you, I can't let you go." I said it like a ham.

She looked up, smiling. Smiling with tears starting in her eyes. "I—just can't believe it, I—" She broke off, sobbing against my chest.

I raised her chin. "Why not?"

"Well, it's just going to sound terribly silly, but I—somehow I kept thinking that some day, *some* day someone would come to Walton. He'd—" She blushed. "I thought of him as my—prince."

"Well, here I am—your prince." (I almost choked on that—*me*, Prince Eric!)

Her eyes were all worship. "You're just like I always pictured you—in every respect. And I couldn't marry a man who wasn't terribly religious—"

"Am I—religious?"

"Of course you are, darling, whether you're aware of it or not. How else in the world could you communicate with the dead if you weren't just terribly close to the Almighty!"

I wondered then if putting up with this would be worth the ten grand.

"Of course I'll marry you, darling!"

"On Saturday?" My voice was weak.

"Good heavens! That's only four days! I've a million little things to do. We'll live right here in Walton, won't we? You won't want to go away some place to live?"

"No. Walton's okay."

"Eric, I saw the most adorable little apartment. I was going to the grocery store and saw the sign, so I looked the place over just out of curiosity. It's right up over the grocery store, at the corner of Lilac and Palm. I could rent it, and we could live there until we decide on a permanent place—"

"Sure," I said, "rent it."

"And I could borrow Mr. Corbitt's trailer for our honeymoon. He has absolutely no use for it, darling. He told me I could take it any time I liked—"

"You mean one of those things they fasten on cars?"

She nodded enthusiastically. "This one's like a little house. It's perfect."

"Sure. Go ahead. Borrow it."

"And—good heavens—we'll have to get the marriage license and the health certifi—" She looked up suddenly and her face colored. "There's just one thing, I—Clara mentioned it when we got home that first day I met you at church. She wondered why you weren't in the army. And I sort of wondered, too—since you're young and terribly sound looking—" She saw my expression.

"Please don't be offended, dear. It's just that when a girl gets married—"

"Yeah, yeah. You want to know why I'm a slacker. Too much scar tissue in my lungs. When I was a kid I had pneumonia seven times."

"Oh, I'm sorry. I imagine it was a dreadful shock when you found out you couldn't serve your country."

"I did feel pretty bad about that," I said.

"I'll explain it all to Clara. Then she'll know it's all right." She paused. "I'm sure Clara won't be nasty to you when she knows we're actually going to be *married!* Let's go tell her right now!"

I hesitated, thinking it over. The farther away I could stay from Clara, the safer I felt. But there was no way around it. Emmie was set on going.

"Sure," I said. "We might as well tell Clara and get it over with."

We got out of the Plymouth. Emmie opened the gate out in front of the house. It was a small, white frame with the porch light on. All the blinds were drawn but light reflected through them.

We went up the curved walk. On the front porch, I heard a radio playing from inside. Emmie slid the bottoms of her shoes over the door mat. I was so nervous I did the same thing. We went inside. The living room was small and drab and as clean as a whistle. The furnishings all had a brownish cast, except the wine rug. There was some kind of dark tan drapery at the windows, and more of this drapery hung in an archway. It prevented you from seeing into the next room. The radio was playing behind it.

"Sit down, darling. I'll go tell Clara you're here." Emmie put her hands on my arms. "I'll tell her first—and break the news gently."

I nodded and she disappeared into the next room. I heard a door open and close. I dropped down on the divan, feeling limp. I was a fish out of water. I felt like making a dive for the door. Any moment I expected Clara to come pouncing through the drapery to accuse me of marrying Emmie for her dough!

I sat there for what seemed an eternity. I strained to hear voices. I heard nothing. No sound from the house. Only the tick of the clock. And the faraway beat of the ocean.

Finally I got up and walked to the window. I examined a small vase on the mantel. I was all nerves over this Clara business. I turned suddenly to go back to the divan. Then I jumped.

Clara was standing just inside the drapery, with her arms folded across her chest. I didn't know how long she'd been there. You could tell she knew the bad news. Her face was all martyrdom. I noticed her skin had a greenish cast under the light. She kept giving me the stare with those small, beady eyes. She gave me the creeps.

"I understand you wish to marry Emmie?" She said it like she was asking if I wanted to buy a fat pig.

"That's right. I love Emmie a lot."

She nodded, then gestured to the divan. "Sit down."

I sat. Emmie came in then with a tray. She poured tea and handed me a cup. She sat on the couch beside me, while Clara sat opposite us in a straight-back chair. With the same sour puss she gazed at me.

We all stirred sugar into our tea, then Clara said:

"Tell me about yourself, Mr. Stanton."

Before I could, she was asking me questions. She was interested in the spiritual part of my life. I put it on thick: told her it was sort of a calling, something like Priesthood. Something you feel that's your life's work.

She asked me where I was born, my mother's maiden name, were my parents living? What diseases had they had? How old was I, what did I do before I became a spiritualist medium? High school or college education? Did I have a bank account, had I been married before?

She made it sound like conversation, but boiled down I thought she was deliberately being obnoxious, hoping she'd scare me out. I kept up a line of running gab, told her lies about everything. I only told the truth when I couldn't think of a lie. That wasn't often. I painted myself a little tin Jesus, talked her under the table. She sat watching me with those vacant eyes, nodding—then suddenly she began to cry.

It was the damnedest thing I ever saw. There were tears in her eyes, but she was sort of whining.

"You have no need to cry," I told her. "I'll be good to Emmie."

She smiled through her tears. "I know you will, Eric. You're a good boy. I'm not worrying about that. It's just that my head hurts so dreadfully."

"Oh, I'm sorry—"

She was eager for sympathy. "I hear noises sometimes," she said. "Noises like airplane motors. And then again it's like an automobile—just starting up." She bit her lip. "It worries me so." Her eyes came up and flickered. "I've been to a doctor. He tells me it's only my imagination." She smiled wearily. "And I know I don't imagine it. That doctor is crazy!"

A sudden chill went up my spine. You only had to look at her eyes to tell. It'd probably been creeping on her gradually: the shock of her husband leaving her had caused it maybe. She was harmless enough, but one of these nights she might kick up her heels. I wouldn't have wanted to sleep in the same house with her.

Clara got up, holding her forehead, and went through the drapery. I walked over to the door and motioned to Emmie. She followed me outside.

Back in the Plymouth, I said:

"Does your sister cry much like that?"

Emmie nodded. "All the time. She gets sick much too often." She paused. "I'm going to make her go see another doctor."

"Did you ever stop to think," I said, "she might be on the verge of insanity?"

She stared at me. "Oh, I'll never think that! Clara's perfectly all right. There's nothing wrong with her. All she needs is some friends. Maybe it's a good thing I'm getting married. She'll be alone and have to get out and meet people. But don't say the other, Eric. It isn't true! Don't ever say it!"

"Okay, okay," I said.

But I kept thinking about it while she drove me back to the hotel. I remembered what Stella had said about both Clara and Emmie having ten thousand bucks. And here Clara was, about ripe for a state institution. Sister Clara was as crazy as a bat. She was dangerously insane!

There must be some way, I thought, to get her to sign over the dough before they put her away in an asylum.

Twenty thousand bucks! That was dough like I'd never seen!

I got my enthusiasm back all right.

8

We were married on Saturday morning. Eleven o'clock at the church, the Reverend Thomas presiding. I had on my dark blue suit—and Emmie wore a shiny blue dress, blue flowers on each side of her hair and that angelic gleam in her eyes.

Clara was there, too, with her headache, and a few of Emmie's girl friends. The preacher gave out with the words, and I slipped a plain gold band on Emmie's finger (five bucks at the local jeweler). I'd already told her that I'd ordered a swell diamond, but it took time for it to be sent from L.A. She was pleased over the idea. But I kept wondering what I was going to tell her later—when the ring didn't come. I could always be plenty sore about it. I could pretend to write letters to the jewelry store—things like that.

When the ceremony was over, I put on a good show for the customers. I kissed Emmie like Mickey Mouse kisses Minnie. And a couple of Emmie's repulsive girl friends kissed me then, including Clara. There was a feeble attempt at rice-throwing while we ran out and hopped in the Plymouth. The trailer was attached to the back of it and there were "Just Married" signs in all the windows.

I piped them and got sick to my stomach.

There was a lot of waving when we started off. Tin cans and old shoes rattling along the pavement. Emmie said she'd forgotten to get gas, so we had to circle down to the main street. We pulled in at a service station and I paid out two more smackers for gas. I was glad we had the trailer: it'd save a hotel bill. I wasn't any too well greased by now. Forty bucks remaining.

We got going finally, cruising down the main street, down toward Pop's Place. Everybody was ogling us, heads sticking out of shop doors and windows, people laughing, cheering us on. I wanted to vanish into thin air! Those goddam tin cans dragging on the bumper drove me nuts!

Then I saw something that really got me going: the black Buick parked out in front of Pop's! I saw the license plates—Arizona. I wanted to jump out the car window—grab that handsome walrus and wipe the street with him! I wanted to grab Stella in my arms and never let her go!

It didn't really hit me until then: Emmie driving me off on a honeymoon—when I was aching for Stella so much I couldn't get my breath.

Right then and there I decided when I got back I'd give that fat walrus the going over—get at him with anything I could get my hands on! He'd stay out of Pop's joint after I finished with him. He'd be lucky if he could even walk!

I thought about him until we were a couple of miles out of town, then I heard the tin cans again. I told Emmie to stop. I got out and jerked them off and took the signs out of the trailer windows. Then we were rolling again. To our right was the ocean.

"Darling, I'm so terribly happy—"

"Me, too." I was about as happy as a guy ready to be guillotined, but I kept a smile on my kisser.

"You'll love it in the trailer camp. It's right off the ocean, and such a nice place, so neatly kept."

"It is?"

"Darling—we'll swim and lie around in the sun for three days."

Three days.... It sounded like three years!

"Wonderful," I said. "Are there horses?"

She laughed. "Heavens, no. Whatever in the world made you think there were horses?"

I wasn't thinking, that was the trouble. "I thought maybe we could go horseback riding."

"At a trailer camp?" She was still laughing.

"No, I guess not."

"But at night we can go grunion hunting," she said.

"Grunion? What kind of hunting is that?"

"You've never heard of grunion? They're little fish. The waves wash them right up on the sand."

A hell of a fine sport, I thought, picking up little fish from the sand!

"Some people use nets."

"They do?"

"Yes, darling. Before the dim-out, they used to build fires on the sand and fry the grunion. They're delicious. We might dig for clams, too."

"There are clams, too?"

"Oh, yes. And I brought frying pans and cooking utensils—and canned supplies."

"I'm glad of that. You must be a wonderful cook."

"Not so very good. But I'll be a good cook for you, darling."

Just before dusk we pulled into the trailer camp. It was down off the main highway. I was wrong about the hotel bill. They collected three bucks at the entrance. Three bucks for three days—just for parking space.

There was a grocery store, and restrooms to one side. Emmie drove on, down past a barbecue pit. There were signs all around it, reminding people not to make fires. We passed other trailers, some with tents attached. People camping out. A couple of fat slobs of women looked at us. A baby was bawling from somewhere. You could hear the ocean more here, even over the grind of the car motor.

Emmie decided the spot to park was between two trees. She pulled in, off the dirt road, away from the other cars. When she turned off the motor, it seemed like we were lost from the world. It was cold and lonely—and the echo of the ocean drummed in my ears.

We went inside the trailer then, and Emmie explained how everything worked. She showed me the icebox and how the oil stove was turned on. She showed me the two couches and how they made up into twin beds. The trailer was compact. As Emmie said over and over: it was just like a little house. I spent a half hour looking it over. Then she told me to put on some old trousers and to take off my shoes and socks.

We were going grunion hunting.

The ocean was a city block away from the trailer. We stood there in the sand, in our bare feet, picking up the slimy, stinking little fish. She had a box ready to put them in. And when she wasn't helping me she was digging for clams. We got six clams and eight fish.

Back in the trailer, she cleaned and fried the fish. She made coffee and sliced some tomatoes. She got out a can of string beans from the cupboard, another of potatoes. She put the clams in boiling water and cut them from their shells. She fried them, too. She pulled down the table top. It was hidden in the wall—like an ironing board.

I was hungry, and the dinner was good.

I remember later that night—Emmie in her yellow satin nightgown, her hair tied back with a ribbon. She'd turned out the lights in the trailer and put up the blinds to let the air in while we slept. I was already in pajamas, in one of the twin beds.

Then Emmie sat down on my bed. She reached over and kissed me below my ear.

"Tired, darling?"

"Yeah, I sure am. I'm all done in."

I pretended to fall asleep then. But I was wide awake, and thinking of Stella. I kept listening to the ocean and thinking of Stella.

In the following three days I developed a minor hatred for Emmie. She was so damned agreeable. I began to wish I'd never seen her. She cooked every meal and washed the dishes right up. She waited on me hand and foot.

When she voiced an opinion and I contradicted her, she'd always side in with my views. I noticed this more and more. She was so anxious to please she robbed herself of any individuality. And then the thought of Stella was constantly gnawing inside me, tormenting me. I gave plenty of thought to the walrus, too, and imagined all sorts of things—like maybe she was down on the sand with him right now. Things like that. Things that almost drove me nuts!

So no wonder in three days' time I was barking at Emmie. But she didn't seem to care or notice. She treated me with the same loving patience I couldn't endure.

I was plenty relieved when we were all packed up again, ready to scram. Emmie pulled out of the camp and then we were on the highway again, rolling. I was so happy at the prospect of seeing Stella, I was amiable to Emmie again.

"I'll be glad when we're settled in the apartment, dear," she said as she drove. "I'm sure you won't be so restless then."

I nodded through a yawn.

"But, Eric—let's buy a house. I've always wanted a lovely little home."

"Sure, sure. We'll look around and find one."

It was coming quicker than I thought. All I needed was those bonds cashed.

"We'd better pay all cash for it," I said.

"Oh, yes—and we'll stay in the apartment only until we find the right house to buy." She smiled happily. "How much money do you want to put into it, dear?"

I felt my throat tighten. "Emmie, *my* money's tied up in stocks. I'd rather not draw it out right now—unless you insist."

"Oh, no," she said quickly. "I'll put *my* money in the house, dear."

I breathed normally again.

"I'll look around for a suitable one," she said. "I'll look next week."

"Yeah. The sooner the better." I thought for a moment. "Let's get a nice house. Put all your dough in it. I'll arrange to draw out some of mine for us to live on."

"Yes," she said, "we'll buy a very nice house."

We were almost into Walton. It was seven-thirty. I asked her to gas up the heap—told her I had to see a guy in town, a guy that had a house for sale.

She let me out in front of the theatre. I told her to leave the stuff in the trailer. I'd pack it out in the morning. She gave me the address of the apartment where we were to live. I hadn't even seen the joint: she'd rented it herself, with her dough.

"It's on the corner of Lilac and Palm," she said. "The only apartment up over the grocery store. You can't miss it."

"Okay. See you a little later."

She drove on.

I forgot it all then. I forgot everything. I was hurrying down to Pop's Place.

9

I was on a raft in mid-ocean, and she was the first sight of land.

I saw her first through the window, putting on a little hat in the mirror. She had on that black dress again. She looked so cute and pretty, the way she was arranging the hat this way and that, I couldn't wait to get inside to her.

I opened the door and went in. I snapped the lock behind me. I grabbed her in my arms and crushed my lips down on hers, lipstick and all. Her hat fell to the floor. I kept kissing her as fast as I could. Kissing her and smelling that perfume.

"Eric—" she kept saying, "— people pass by! People'll see you!"

She finally brushed me off and put her hands on her hips. "Now what's this all about?"

I laughed. "Can't a guy be glad to see you, honey?"

She picked up her hat from the floor. "Well, you don't have to muss me all up! You act like you been having gland treatments!"

"What the hell you talking about?" I wiped the grin from my face.

Her nose tilted up. "It must be nice—lying around in the sun with your wife—getting a tan like that."

I caught my reflection in the mirror. "I'm sunburned." It was the first time I knew it.

"By the way, how *is* Mrs. Stanton?"

"Stella, don't be like that."

She straightened. "Can't I ask you a few questions about your wife?"

"Listen—"

"I don't see how you could stand her. I saw her just that once at the séance. She didn't have much make-up on her face. Is she too good to wear make-up? I don't see how you could stand that pale look—"

"I couldn't. That's what I've been trying to tell you. I'm nuts about you. I can't—"

"I'll bet! I'll bet that trailer was some love nest! I saw you and Emmie driving off, both of you in seventh heaven—"

My face dropped. "Stella, all I've been doing is aching my guts out for you."

"Yeah. I'll bet!"

"Listen to me—"

"I've finished listening. You and me are through!"

"Don't be jealous, honey. We both agreed to this. You said—"

"I said a lot of things. But I been thinking. I been thinking a lot. Especially about how dumb I am. I'm the one that's the sucker. Not Emmie. She's got the ring on her finger. What have I got? *Just what have I got?* A promise. A promise that don't mean a damned thing!" She turned and began putting on her hat again. "No, the deal's off!"

I stood there, staring. There was an awful ache inside me. I was weak. My voice was weak:

"Don't say that, honey."

"I mean it—I'm through!"

"Stella, all those plans we made. I wouldn't have married Emmie if you hadn't said it was all right yourself. I don't want her money. It's for you. You've got to believe me, it's the truth! I—"

"Oh, sure—"

"Listen, I'm no cluck. I knew I couldn't keep a girl like you if I didn't have dough—"

"You're absolutely right!" She shook her head. "But I'm not waiting for you to get tired of Emmie Barkley!"

"You don't make sense! We—"

"We were out of our heads, that's what we were. We were pipe-dreaming. But I woke up. And I'm through. I must've been crazy to say I'd go away with you. I wouldn't. Not for ten million dollars. I'd stay clear of any man who'd do anything like that!" She turned back to me; her eyes narrowed. "You're nothing but a blackmailer—a dirty extortionist!"

"Listen—"

"You can get sent up for extortion. Plenty years in jail." She put her hands on her hips again and threw back her head. "You think *I'm* going to get sent up? Huh-uh. Not on your life. Count me out!"

She shook her head again. I saw her glance to the window. My eyes followed. I caught a glimpse of the Buick, just driving away from the curb. It hit me smack in the face!

The walrus had been watching us. I wondered why Stella'd been shaking her head so much. Now I knew. It was to tell him not to come in. The dress hit me, too, and the perfume. She was all fixed up to go out with the walrus! She'd fallen for him! She was pushing me out a ten-story window. I was so weak I had to go over to the counter and sit down.

"Your wife's probably waiting for you," she went on. "Go on home. Be a nice little husband. But don't come back here or I'll spill the whole thing to Emmie. I'm fed up with everything. This town's a jinx. I don't like this town. And I'm getting out. Maybe even tonight yet. But regardless of when I go, I don't want to see you again. I'm dead serious, Eric. When I'm through I'm through!"

I got up. Somehow I walked to the front. I opened the door and went outside. I stayed in the shadows of the buildings and waited. In a few minutes the coupe rolled up again. The lights in Pop's Place went out. Stella came outside. She hurried over to the Buick and got in.

"We better clear out of here fast," I heard her saying.

The car sped off.

I walked slowly to the corner of Lilac and Palm. I went up the steps at the side of the grocery store. Emmie opened the door and said:

"This isn't fair, darling. I wanted to be carried across the threshold."

She tried to kiss me. I brushed on past her. She showed me through the apartment, but I didn't see it. She said that only one thing had bothered her. She hadn't been able to find the key to a closet door in the kitchen. And when she finally located it, she discovered something.

It wasn't a closet at all, she said, but a stairway leading down to the grocery store.

She said: "The grocery man used to live up here. But he told me since his progeny increased to three—he had to find larger living quarters. He bought a spacious house, darling, on Elm Street."

She kept on talking. Said something about the place would be quite livable when she put up some decent drapes. That it was nice and secluded, and I said yeah it was.

She had dinner waiting, but I didn't eat. I went downstairs, to the trailer, and got two pints of whiskey. I brought the bottles back up. I drank them both, and the ache in my guts went away somewhat. I say somewhat, because you have no idea what a down-in-the-mouth bastard I was. The bottom had dropped out of everything. The words Stella said were still pounding inside me. I was sick and sore and trembling.

I was on my raft again....

I went into the bedroom. There was one double bed. I sat on it and rested my head on the headboard to keep it from hurting so much. Emmie came in then to see if I was all right. My bleary eyes focused on her:

"Emmie ..."

"Yes, darling?"

"Come to bed."

I remember later that night. Emmie was sound asleep. I got out of bed and put on my clothes. I went downstairs. Then I was walking.

The streets were dark and dismal, and the cold air stung my face. In the distance, the orchestra of the sea beat out its odd, jumbled jive.

I kept on walking. When I got back to the apartment the clock said five. Emmie was still asleep.

10

"You tell that crazy sister of yours to keep out of my way!"

"But, Eric—Clara didn't mean to see you. She was just walking along there last evening—in front of that restaurant. And she saw you—through the window—kissing that girl."

"She saw somebody else!"

"That's what I told her, dear. But Clara insisted it was you. She said she waited until early this morning to tell me, instead of last night, because she thought it would be such a shock to me."

I got out of bed. I went into the bathroom. My head was splitting. Outside the windows the sun was bright. It was ten, maybe eleven o'clock. I'd been sleeping that long. I said:

"So now I haven't anything to do but go around kissing waitresses—"

Emmie had followed me into the bathroom. I took off my clothes and got in the tub. I closed the sliding shower door, but she still stood there.

"It seems so incredible, darling—when we've only been married four days."

"That sister of yours is trying to cause trouble—that's how her twisted mind works! She didn't see anything like that. I tell you she ought to be locked up somewhere!"

"Don't say that, darling. Please don't. Ever again. Please. And don't swear, dear. It doesn't become you." She paused. "Clara *thought* she saw you—so naturally she told me. That's only being sisterly."

"So she's already beginning to cook up things to get me in dutch, is she? So that's her scheme, is it?" I turned on the shower to drown Emmie's voice. But I could hear it just the same:

"It's really terribly serious—because that young girl was found dead this morning—"

I had turned on the hot water. My hands went too numb to turn on the cold. I just stood there, with that scalding water searing my flesh.

"Say that again, Emmie."

"The waitress in that restaurant was found dead this morning, dear. I went to see her, after what Clara told me this morning. I wanted to make sure it wasn't you who saw her last night. I intended to ask her. But I couldn't, because there were police in the place and the old man who owns the restaurant was crying so pitifully. And she was dead on a cot in the kitchen. I saw her. It wasn't a pretty sight. Her head had been—"

"*Shuddup, Emmie!*"

I jumped out of the tub. I threw a towel around me. I was burning all over and my teeth were chattering. I grabbed Emmie by the shoulders. "She's *dead?* She's really dead? *Don't lie to me!*"

"I'm not lying, dear. She was dead when I got there."

I went into the bedroom and tried to find my clothes. I kept going over to the window and looking out, I don't know why. I couldn't find my clothes. Emmie came in and handed them to me from the chair. Somehow I got them on. I ran down the steps to the street. I still didn't believe Stella was dead.

I thought: *That goddam Emmie lied to me!*

But I noticed everything was still. The air was still and the trees were still. Nothing was moving, and suddenly the sun was hiding behind a dark cloud.

There was a motorcycle out in front—a cop's motorcycle. There were people gathered on the sidewalk—asking each other what happened. I went past them, up to the door. It was locked. I saw a cop inside, walking toward me. He was a big cop. I started to get the shakes. He opened the door a little and asked me what I wanted. I pushed the door open. It threw him back against the wall. I got inside and started to the back. The cop made a lunge: he whirled me around by the collar with his fist all doubled up, ready.

"It's all right," Pop's voice came from somewhere, "it's Mr. Stanton."

The cop let go of my collar and started looking me over, with his fist still doubled. I turned away and moved on to the back. In the doorway I stopped and then my throat was so tight I couldn't swallow.

She had on the black dress—only it was ripped at the neck, and her hair was dark on one side where the blood had dried. There were more dark blotches on the pillow of the cot where her head was lying, and some on the cement.

"She got it bad—"

There were two guys standing beside her, and it was one of them who'd spoken. I didn't know whether it was the cop or the little guy who was putting shiny instruments back into a satchel.

I found my voice: "What killed her?"

The cop said: "The coroner here says she was hit with a blunt instrument."

The coroner looked up at me and nodded. "It could have been anything," he said. "One severe blow. It got her on the right temple—must have hit the middle meningeal artery." He looked down to Stella. "She was killed after four o'clock this morning. Everything indicates there must have been a, struggle—"

I kept staring. The room blurred for a moment. Then I saw her again. I wanted to go over and kneel beside her. I wanted to kiss the clean side of her hair and her lips. I wanted to tell her things I'd never told her before. But this cop was watching....

"You look like you're going to faint, bud—" He took my arm and led me out. He swung one of the counter chairs around and sat me down.

"What's your name?"

"Stanton. Eric Stanton."

"Stella Flint was a girl friend of yours?"

"That's right. Just a friend."

"Well, you just sit here, Mr. Stanton, until you feel better."

"Thanks...."

He went into the back again. I saw Pop then, sitting up at the counter by the window. He was dabbing a dirty white apron to his eyes. I got up and sat down beside him. His eyes were all red-rimmed, and tears were falling off his face. Suddenly he clutched his hands on my jacket lapels:

"Who killed her, Eric?"

I couldn't answer. I swallowed hard.

"You're with the F.B.I.! You can find out who killed her!"

I began to sweat. "Listen, Pop—I'm no F.B.I. man. I only told you that. I was kidding. Get it? It was a joke."

He let go of my coat and stared at me.

I was talking low, so the guys in the back couldn't hear. Even the cop who'd been at the door was back there now. "Do me a favor, Pop. Don't go telling any of these cops I told you that. They wouldn't understand it was a joke."

"I already told one," he said. "He isn't here now. He was here this mornin'. He's a big cop, sort of flabby-faced. He doesn't wear a uniform. He comes in here and drinks soda pop most every afternoon—but I didn't know he was a cop. I told him. I said, 'Mr. Stanton will find out who killed her 'cause he's with the F.B.I.'"

"What did the cop say?"

"Nothin'. He just wrote down your name in a little black book."

"Well, don't tell anybody else."

"I won't, Eric. But who could have done this thing?"

"I got my suspicions," I said. "And I'd like to find him just once. I think it was the walrus—the one she was out with last night. The guy that has the black Buick coupe."

Pop's eyes flicked up. "I didn't like that one's looks. I told Stella he was a bad one. He carries a gun, Eric. But Stella said she'd known him a long time, so I didn't."

"She knew this guy *before*, Pop?"

"That's what she said—"

"Who is he?"

"I ain't got the slightest idea. When I told the cop about him, he wanted to know who he was, too. But I couldn't tell him, 'cause I don't know. All I could tell him was that he drove a black coupe. The cop went away then and when he came back he told me the man's name was Dave Watkins— or Atkins, I think he said. He'd checked at the hotel where the fella' stayed."

"The cop arrested him?"

Pop shook his head. "He's nowheres in town. But the cop found out his name at the hotel. He checked out early last night, and nobody knows where he went."

"I'd like to get my hands on him," I said.

"Me, too," Pop said. "But the big cop told me he'd have him back here within twenty-four hours—"

"He killed her all right."

"I guess so, Eric." He paused. "But what was she doin' back here in the restaurant? Why should she come back once she'd gone out? And it was late. About four o'clock this morning. Why'd she have to come back—and get killed?"

I shrugged. I couldn't talk. I was too choked up.

Pop's shoulders slumped and then his head drooped into his arms on the counter and pretty soon he was bawling again. I couldn't stand it. He had me wanting to do it. I got up and went outside. I didn't say good-bye or go-to-hell to the cops. I just walked out.

Stella was dead.

When I got home the apartment had a gloomy atmosphere. It was always clean, neat at a pin, and today was no exception, but there was a tenseness in the room, a bleakness—or maybe it was me. I felt dazed. I stood limp, half-wondering where Emmie was. I heard a scraping noise from the kitchen. I hurried across the carpet, through the dining room, and paused in the kitchen doorway.

Emmie stood before the sink, her hands in soapy dishwater. I could only see her profile—but I saw that her eyes were closed, tears streaming down her face. There was a stack of dishes piled on one side ready to be washed. There were glasses in the dishpan, but Emmie's hands were motionless.

"What's wrong?" My voice wasn't natural: I knew what was wrong all right. Stella. In the next few minutes I would have to graduate into professional acting. I was pretty good at it, only I was what is known as a hot-air artist.

Emmie didn't look up. She kept her eyes straight ahead. "You knew that—waitress—didn't you?"

It was the last thing I wanted to talk about. "Yeah," I said.

She started to sob. My feet carried me over to her, and I stood behind her with my arms around her waist, trying to calm her. I didn't want to see her eyes.

"Did—you—love—her?"

I kissed the back of her neck. It made me feel foolish. "If I loved her—why'd I marry you?"

She stopped crying and thought about that. I felt her body tightening.

"Then it was you Clara saw last night...."

"Well—you know how it is." It was a feeble attempt. "The kid, she—she was stuck on me. And she asked me to kiss her good-bye. You see, I took her out a couple times—a movie or two—see? I was lonely and—I guess I felt kind of sorry for her—an ordinary waitress. And I guess I was sort of infatuated, in a mild degree. But when I met you I dropped her flat."

Emmie turned around. She dried her hands on a dish towel and wiped her tears away with the back of her hand. She looked up at me then, with new hope. "Tell me everything," she said breathlessly.

I kept my gaze on the pile of dirty silverware on the sink and fished around for the words:

"Well—you see, Pop Elliot wasn't in the restaurant last night, so I couldn't ask him about a house to buy—so naturally I had to say a few words to Stella. And before I knew it she was crying. She said it was because I got married. She said, 'Will you kiss me good-bye?' I said, 'No, Stella—it wouldn't be right to my bride—'"

I kept a straight face while I said it, and suddenly I was thinking about what Stella'd really said: *Go on home! Don't come back anymore. I'm fed up with everything. This town's a jinx. I'm getting out. Maybe even tonight yet. But regardless of when I go, I don't want to see you. I'm dead serious, Eric—when I'm through I'm through!*

"You said *that*, darling? You said it wouldn't be right to your bride?"

"Yeah. That's what I told her. And the poor kid kept standing there with those big tears in her eyes. She said, 'This is the end, the last time I'll ever see you and you won't even kiss me good-bye?' Then she cried some more." I stirred. "Oh, hell—in plain words—I felt sorry for the kid and kissed her good-bye. I know I shouldn't have—but I did."

"Of *course* you should!"

I looked at Emmie quickly wondering if I'd heard right. She was smiling. I'd never seen her face so happy.

"That was the nicest thing you could do. I don't feel badly about it at all—now that I know. The poor girl, she—" Her eyes clouded. "And now she's been murdered. How horrible."

"Yeah," I said. "Horrible is the word all right." A lump was working up and down in my throat—like an elevator.

11

They didn't waste time. The burial was the very next day. Her mother wasn't there. Her mother was notified and she sent a telegram to Pop—from Arizona, expressing her grief and regrets. But I was at the funeral, and Pop was. A preacher was there, because Pop paid out three hundred bucks for the burial services. And a few of the townspeople were curious, so they were there.

They lowered her in the grave, but I didn't watch that part of the service. Pop was bawling again, and I couldn't stand to hear him. I glanced back just once, though, and saw them shoveling the dirt over.

I left the graveyard and wandered all around town. I walked past the church and down to the ocean. I sat on the sand a long time, trying to think, to figure things out. But my mind was a vacuum. I couldn't think or feel. Stella was dead, and it occurred to me suddenly that I must be dead too. I began to laugh, sitting by myself there on the sand, laughing like hell because I was dead too.

Sure, I'd known girls before. Plenty. Blondes, brunettes and redheads. There was one little carrot-haired burlesque dancer in L.A. who had me going for a while. But when she gave me the cold shoulder, did I worry? I laughed it off. I didn't care one way or the other. But with Stella—well, she was great.

Anyway, I sat there trying to comb the cobwebs out of my brain. I wondered what my next move should be. Maybe the best thing for me would be to get on the move, damned fast....

But Stella had been murdered, and they were looking for the killer. The local police were all a dither. You'd be surprised what a scare the whole affair threw into the town. There weren't any women or kids on the streets after dark and when you walked past the shops in the daytime you'd always hear little groups whispering.

The local paper spilled it all over the front page. It made headlines, above the war. Some hack columnist went crazy on it.

Called it the *Bludgeon Murder*. He said that no one in town could sleep soundly again until the demented fiend had been found. He used words like that.

They published Stella's picture and underneath it asked if anyone had seen this girl on the night of September 28. If so, would they get in touch with the police. It told of a few people who'd already reported to the cops.

A guy who owned the Blue Lantern Café, about a mile out of town, said he'd seen Stella's picture, and that she was the girl who was in his place about nine o'clock with a well-dressed man. It went on describing the walrus to a T. The café man said Stella and the guy sat there drinking and arguing. He said he was too busy to pay much attention. But the man kept asking her to go somewhere and the girl kept refusing. Once Stella got up and started out the door, but the man ran after her and brought her back. They left his place around nine-thirty.

Then a woman who lives right off the highway said she was reading in her front room at approximately ten-thirty on the murder night and heard arguing out in front. She went out on the front porch and noticed a dark coupe parked off the highway, about fifty feet from her house. She saw a young blonde girl getting out of the car and running. The girl stumbled and the man caught up with her. The girl said: "Now I've torn my dress." She said they talked for a while then, and she saw them kissing. So she figured it was only a lover's quarrel and wasn't alarmed.

The paper also published a picture of the landlady at the rooming house where Stella lived. Her name was Florence Henderson. She said her bedroom was right off the front porch. Around twelve o'clock on the murder night she was awakened by a car stopping out in front. She thought it was her husband coming home from his night shift at the factory. But when he didn't come in the house she got up out of bed and looked out the window. She saw a black coupe parked under the streetlamp in front. A man opened the door and Stella got out. She said she didn't notice what he looked like, except he was heavy set. She thought nothing of it and got back in bed. She heard a car start off and then stop. Then Stella's voice: "What do you want now?"

That was all Stella said. The landlady was positive it was

Stella Flint because she had only one other girl roomer, a southern girl with the accent. But she heard *no other voice*. She couldn't say if Stella'd been talking to a man or a woman. She heard footsteps then, but couldn't remember whether or not she heard a car motor start up again. She said she was worried about her husband and didn't pay much attention. But it sounded like the man had left Stella out in front, then stopped the car and ran back to tell her something. After that the two of them got back in the car and drove off. That was the way it sounded to her.

So you see, everything pointed to the walrus.

I sat there thinking about all this, and the picture of Pop's kitchen in the paper. It had big black letters at the top of it, saying "Murder Kitchen." I remembered how it said the cops had combed the restaurant with a fine-tooth comb. They'd found clues and prints and it was only a matter of time.

Some artist drew a picture of Atkins. He'd never seen him, he'd only had Pop and the hotel owner, where Atkins had stayed, describe him. But it was a pretty good job. It resembled the walrus a lot.

The papers said a dragnet had been spread and all that. But what if they couldn't find Atkins? What if I started making tracks out of town? It might throw suspicion on me. Maybe the best thing I could do was sit tight until the mess cooled. Besides, I hadn't lost interest in the Barkley sisters' twenty thousand bucks. Hell, I'd spent this much time. I might as well see it out.

I was shivering suddenly. The sun was sinking in the west. It was splinters of orange all across the sky. I saw that the tide was moving out fast. The wind was icy cold.

It was beginning to get dark. I got up quick and brushed the sand from my trousers. Then I was moving toward Lilac and Palm.

I went up the steps, without making any noise I guess. Because when I turned the key in the lock and opened the door, Emmie was startled. She was sitting in the easy chair under a floor lamp. She wasn't reading. She looked like she'd been sitting there, staring into space, thinking for a long time.

"Oh, it's you—"

"Yeah." I closed the door behind me, and went over and stood by her chair.

"I was waiting dinner for you."

"I'm not so hungry."

"Nor I," she said.

I noticed that her voice was strained. She was working her hand at the side of her hair, trying to act calm. But something was eating on her. I could feel it. I didn't mince words:

"What's up?"

She hesitated. Her eyes got big and worried. "There's been a man here looking for you. He said he'd be back later."

"What kind of a man?"

She was avoiding my eyes. "Well—I really don't know, he—he only said that he'd be back later. His name was Mark Judd. He showed me a deputy badge, so he must be a policeman." Her voice grew slow and deliberate. "What could a policeman want of you, dear?"

I shrugged, but I was keyed up. The room was suddenly electric. "Did you tell him?"

"Tell him?" She studied me strangely.

"Yes!" I was rattled. "You know what I mean—about what Clara saw—about me, kissing the waitress." My breath was coming in a muffled wheeze.

She kept looking at me.

"You didn't tell him, did you? For God's sake, did you?"

"Eric, I—I didn't talk to the man at all—except to tell him you weren't home."

"You're *sure?* You didn't give him any information?"

Her eyes went to the floor. "None. Not at all. He—he was such a—He was big and soft-looking, and his eyes were—well—"

I remembered what Pop had said: about the cop he'd told I was an F.B.I. man. Pop had described him the way Emmie did now—a big, flabby guy.

"—Now when I think of him," Emmie went on, "there was something unhealthy about him. Like—like I don't know what."

"Yeah. Most cops look like that." I threw the line away, but I was plenty scared. "Forget it, Emmie. He's only a dumb Walton cop."

"I—don't think so, dear. I've never seen him in town." Her eyes came up. "They—haven't found Stella Flint's murderer yet, have they?"

"No."

She was sobbing suddenly. "What *could* he want of you! Why was he so *inquisitive!*"

"Emmie—you said you didn't talk to him." My voice was hollow and faraway.

She buried her face in her hands. "I lied to you. He questioned me all afternoon. He asked me not to tell you he'd talked to me. I don't know why I promised him I wouldn't. He just had a way of—"

"Then you *did* tell him?" I felt choked.

Her head came up. "About your kissing that girl? Oh, no. I wouldn't want a thing like that to get around town. It would be too *embarrassing!* I couldn't live it down—if any of my friends knew you kissed that waitress right after our honeymoon! And I made Clara promise not to tell it to a soul!"

"I want the truth."

"Why, people in this town are too narrow-minded to understand you were only kissing her *good-bye!* Don't you see, it's something they could gossip about forever—I couldn't hold my head up." She was indignant. "Of course I didn't tell him!"

It sounded screwy, I'll admit, but it was calculable. To the long hairs of this burg, murder wasn't half as important as their reputations. An innocent guy would hang before a witness, able to save him, would blemish his own good name in doing so.

"Then Clara hasn't told him either?" I said. "You sure of that?"

"Oh, yes—Clara won't breathe it to a soul. She wouldn't want people to know any more than I would."

I relaxed a little. "It was nice of you to tell Clara that, because I'm going to tell the cops, if they ask me, that I was in the restaurant earlier that night to see Pop. I'm not going to mention I kissed Stella good-bye."

"That's right. Please don't tell them. I couldn't face my friends again if they knew!"

"Then what did you and the cop talk about?"

"He—he asked me all sorts of questions. If you were a special investigator. Why would he ask me such a thing as *that?*" She looked at me.

"It was only a joke I had with the restaurant man." My voice was thin.

"He wanted to know how long I'd known you, what kind of work you did ..."

"What'd you tell him?"

"Naturally I said I'd only known you a few weeks, that you had a very fine reputation as a spiritual medium in Los Angeles—that you came here on a vacation—and we'd met and fallen in love. And in a month or so—you might start practicing here in Walton. I only told him the truth, dear."

The truth! Jesus!

"What else did you talk about?"

"He—asked me about the night before last. I told him how we got back from our honeymoon, how we went to bed early—that you were beside me all night long."

"You told him that? And what'd he say?"

"He asked me to think hard. To try and remember if you were beside me *all night long*." Her mouth quivered. "I—told him about the dream."

"You had a dream?" My heart skipped a beat.

She nodded. "I dreamed I awakened and you weren't there beside me."

"You told Mister Judd that?"

She sniffled up at me. "Yes. He kept asking me to think hard, that maybe it wasn't a dream. To think very hard. I kept telling him over and over that I woke up and you *were there*." Her face paled. "I told him you were there, Eric." She stared at me. "Where did you go in the middle of the night?"

"What—what d'ya mean?"

"I awakened and you weren't there. I looked all over for you."

I felt cold suddenly. "I took a walk. I was jumpy. Hell, it was the whiskey.... I had to settle my nerves." My voice lowered. "Did you tell the cop I went out?"

"No. I couldn't. He—he'd think you killed her. I had to lie to him about the dream because he said, 'If you were asleep, how'd you know your husband was there all night?' So I told him the dream woke me up. That's how I knew you were there."

"Yeah. I'm glad you didn't tell him." I was trembling all of a sudden. "It would've made things look pretty bad for me."

"I slipped on a coat," she said abruptly, "and went outside looking for you. But it was so cold, and—I came back and got in bed." She paused. "But I didn't tell the policeman that, either. He left and said he'd be back tonight."

"What else did you tell him?"

"There was nothing else to tell, dear."

"That's right—nothing else to tell."

She came over to me, searching my eyes, her face pained. "He sounded like he suspected you were connected some way with that murder."

A shiver went down my spine. "No, Emmie, you shouldn't think that. He only asked you the routine questions. They've talked to everybody who knew Stella Flint. They're just getting around to me. You see, they've got to check every angle. He doesn't suspect me at all. It's only a routine checkup."

She was smiling suddenly. "Is that what it was?" Her voice was all relief.

"I'm sure of it."

She reached up and kissed me. Then she was laughing and crying, both at the same time. "How stupid of me to have thought what I did! How utterly stupid!"

"Yeah."

"As if *you* were capable of such a thing! It would take a beast, some kind of a horrible monster to commit such a crime!"

"It sure would."

"And you're such a sweet, gentle, lovable person! I told Mister Judd that, darling. I said, 'My husband is a sweet, fine person!'" She kept kissing me and talking. "I know you were infatuated with that waitress, but darling—you *married* me! That has to prove something! You were fond of that girl, but you fell in *love* with me! That's the way it was, wasn't it?"

"That's right. Just like I said."

She kissed me again. "I'm glad you told me about her. I'm not a bit angry. It just brings us closer together. At first I had such awful torment about it—because you *did* deny it at first, darling. But let's always tell each other the truth—about everything. I'm *glad* you told me! Will you, darling, *always* tell me the truth?"

"Sure."

"Oh, I love you so! I couldn't believe even a little thing bad about you." She put her arms up around my neck. "This may sound dreadful—but I'm almost *glad* that girl is dead. Now we can—"

"Don't say that, Emmie!"

"I can't help it, I *am* glad! When that policeman comes back tonight I'm going to tell him you're not home."

"No, I'll see him. You get dinner on the table to make things look good. We got to show Mister Judd we're not a bit ruffled by his visit."

But I kept thinking: what the hell was Judd's idea crawling around behind my back!

What's he got up his sleeve!

Half an hour later the knock sounded on the door. Sharp and insistent. Emmie looked at me meaningly from across the dinner table. She rose quickly and went into the bedroom. I heard her close the door. I waited a moment, then I got up and crossed through the living room. I turned the knob.

"Stanton?"

I got a flash of the badge. I saw the slouched hat.

"Yeah. Come right on in. I've been waiting for you, Mister Judd."

12

I got a good look at him under the living room light. He was like Pop and Emmie described him: flabby and soft. He wasn't really fat, but he gave that impression. He showed evidence of having recently lost weight: his cheeks sort of hung loose on his face—like a bull dog, and I noticed the brown suit he was wearing was baggy. A dull gold key chain ornamented the unpressed trousers, and the edges of his white shirt cuffs were dirty. There was nothing tidy about the guy. He wore his tie like it was choking him. You could see the collar pin.

His hands were big and red. He wore a big onyx ring. He had big lips, a round bulbous nose, heavy eyebrows over thick-rimmed glasses. You could barely see the pupils of his eyes. He must have been near-sighted: he stood too close to me, looking me over. So close I could feel his breath on my face. It smelled like medicine.

"You're Eric Stanton?" His voice was nasal.

"Yeah." I was nervous all of a sudden. "Won't you sit down, Mister Judd?"

He looked at me again and sat over in the easy chair. He held his hat in one hand, put the other on the arm of the chair. I could hear his heavy breathing clear across the room. It was like he had adenoids. He kept his mouth parted slightly—like that was the only way he could breathe—through his mouth.

I said: "I understand you talked to my wife."

"I thought she'd tell you," he said in a flat, toneless voice. "The quickest and clearest way to get a message across is to tell a woman and instruct her not to tell." He paused. "That always makes her remember it better. She attaches more significance to it."

I managed to grin. "That's a pretty good way of reasoning. I guess women are—" My voice died away. He wasn't listening to me. His eyes were squinting up at the flower design on the wallpaper. Then he was sort of leering at everything in the apartment, with an open air of arrogance.

"You knew Stella Flint rather well?" he said, still inspecting the room.

I glanced at the bedroom door, remembering Emmie was inside there. I wondered if she had her ear to the keyhole. "Rather well? I wouldn't say that. I've been out with Stella a few times, sure."

He nodded and took a cigarette out of his pocket and lighted it. "That's what I mean. When was the last time you saw her alive?"

I was all ready for that one. I gave it to him fast. "Eight o'clock on the night she was murdered. You see, I went to the restaurant looking for Pop Elliot. I wanted to ask him if he knew of a house to buy. But he wasn't there. So I shot the breeze with the waitress for a minute or two." I paused. "Oh, yes—out in front I saw her get in the black coupe with the walrus."

"Walrus?" He screwed up his face like he'd swallowed something he didn't like.

"Dave Atkins," I said. "I didn't know his name at the time."

He yawned and rubbed a hand down over his face. He acted tired, and bored. He looked at the ring on his finger. I sat there on the edge of my chair, waiting for the next question.

"Then you were planning on settling here in Walton."

"Oh, sure," I said. "My wife and I are looking for a little house to buy—just an ordinary house—for ordinary people." I thought saying that was pretty cute. It showed him I was the home type.

He put his eyes back on me. "Didn't your wife inherit money not long ago?"

He had me scared there for a second, but I remembered that everybody in town knew Emmie had that dough, so it wasn't unusual for Judd to ask. Besides he said it in such an offhand manner I didn't think he was trying to trick me. I glanced at the bedroom door again.

"Around ten thousand bucks," I said.

"Nice."

"Yeah. Every little bit helps. Hell, you know how it is with a wife...."

He looked at his fingernails. "No, I don't know how it is with a wife. I've never been married. How is it?"

"Well, you—you plan on having kids, then you got to plan on sending them to college, things like that—"

My nerves were relaxing. I was doing okay with him—shooting

the answers back in a breezy way. I wasn't scared of this dumb Walton cop any longer. I was still going to get my hands on Emmie's dough if it was the last thing I did. My mind was made up to that! It was a good thing my eyes didn't reflect what was behind them.

I heard him say, "Your wife's new, isn't she?"

"New?" This cop was a character. I smiled. "She's new all right. We've been married almost a week. We were having a little anniversary dinner." I glanced at the bedroom door again.

"Then you didn't see Stella at all—later on?"

"No, I sure didn't. In fact I was still on my honeymoon."

There was a silence while I was conscious of his heavy breathing again. The guy was plenty slow-witted, I thought. I'd been prepared to have questions shot at me, like cops do in the movies, but Judd was taking it easy, like his mind was groggy. But I noticed his eyes looked wide awake, shining behind those glasses.

"Have you any idea why she went back to the restaurant?"

I had an idea all right, but I know when to keep my mouth shut. I said, "No, sir, I haven't."

He tapped his fingers together in thought. "I'd like to know if it was Atkins or who it was in there with her. I have a hunch—"

I came in quick. "There isn't any doubt but what it was Atkins, is there?"

He sat up on the edge of the chair and peered over at me. His eyes behind the glasses gave me the creeps.

"We've no proof it was. It could be the Mexican we're holding. Some bum made the mistake of wandering into town night before last. He could've seen the lights on in Pop's Place—"

"Sure," I blurted.

He shrugged. "But common sense says the Mexican is clean. There was a twenty-dollar bill in her purse when we found her. Now the bum would've robbed her, at least." He paused. "No, my hunch says it was somebody who knew her—" He fumbled in his pocket and brought out some papers. He held them under the light, almost up to his nose, while he sorted through them and selected one.

"This report throws a bad light on Ben Elliot."

"On *Pop?*"

He nodded. "Ever see any of the expensive jewelry she wore?"

"Hell, no, I— Yeah, she had on a watch one night. She said the diamonds were real."

"She was telling the truth. I went through all her personal stuff. She had nice jewelry. She had bottle after bottle of perfume: Sweet Sin. All of it." He coughed. "Know how much a bottle of that costs? Twenty-six dollars and forty-five cents, including tax. For only two drams. Now where do you spose she got money for stuff like that?"

"I couldn't imagine, Mister Judd. I didn't buy it."

"I know you didn't." He put the papers back in his pocket, then drew a long drag off his cigarette and stubbed it out. "I found a couple sales slips from the drugstore among her personal things. When I checked the druggist told me he'd ordered the perfume regularly from San Francisco—special orders for Ben Elliot—"

"*Pop* bought her the stuff? That's ridiculous!"

He ignored me. "I'm still checking on the jewelry. It wasn't purchased here in town—but chances are Elliot got that for her too."

"Why the hell should *he*—"

His eyes leered at me. "Because she strung him along, that's why."

My voice lowered. "I don't believe it!"

A smile played on his lips. "I'm not saying he was her friend—understand—like you were her friend. I'm saying the guy had hopes—even at his age."

"I'll be damned! You sure can never tell about people!"

"No, you never can."

I gulped down a breath. "Pop took her death pretty hard. You don't suppose *he*—"

Judd settled back. "That's what I came here to ask you. I have respect for the F.B.I." He was smiling to himself.

My stomach sank. "Cut it out, Mister Judd. That was only a joke between me and Pop." I glanced at the bedroom door.

His eyes were on me. "I figured as much. Only you shouldn't go around joking like that, Stanton. Jokes like that lead you to a cell in San Quentin."

"Yeah. That was one hell of a poor joke."

He sat up. "I knew you weren't with the F.B.I., I checked on that.

I knew you're in the spook business. That's interesting." He sucked in a breath. "But somehow you don't strike me as being a séancer. You strike me as being an insurance dick who knocks down plenty on the side. And a smart one, mind you. A guy who works so smart he can get nothing pinned on him. All that could happen would be the sheriff showing you the way out of Los Angeles and instructing you never to show your face there again!"

I was shaking inside. My eyes were on the bedroom door again. I lowered my voice to a hoarse whisper. "All right, Mister Judd—so you checked on that, too. Hell, you must understand how it is. I decided to turn over a new leaf. I had to tell my wife I was in *some* kind of business!"

I got another jolt then thinking: Christ! There goes my ten thousand bucks in smoke! If Emmie had her ear glued to what we were saying, the show was over. I began to get sore. If this dumb cop made me let anything else out of the bag I'd smack my fist down his throat!

"Sure," he said, "I understand how it is. Well—" he went on slowly, "I figure we'll have Dave Atkins back before tomorrow night. He's bound to be picked up by then. 'Course it's only another one of my hunches, but—"

I was scared. I said: "I'd like to get my hands around that throat of his just once. I'd like to—"

Judd cackled a laugh. I looked over at him puzzled. "Ever been to Hollywood, Stanton?"

I didn't get it. I was plenty disgusted with this bird all at once. "Sure. So what?"

"So nothing. They've got some slick actors out there. 'Course I like a Broadway play. New York—that's my home."

I thought: if he thinks I'm going to sit here discussing Old Home Week—he's nuts! I said: "I thought we were talking about Stella Flint."

"We are," he said. "We're still on that subject." He paused. "By the way—are you okay with the draft board?"

I reached in my hip pocket and brought out my card. I got up and handed it to him.

"Hell," I said, "there's nothing I'd rather do than be in on the fight—but look there, Mister Judd. The army examiners said they never saw such lungs as mine. I had pneumonia seven times when I was a kid."

He held the card up to his eyes, then handed it back to me.

"You a Walton cop?" I asked him.

He laughed, then he got up and stood by the chair. "I am now. I got a sister here in Walton—so I came here. It so happens I'm a sick man. The doctors told me I had to have an ocean climate."

"I'm sorry to hear that."

I saw he was ready to leave. He picked up his hat and held it in his hands. I went over to the door and opened it. He still stood by the chair, looking at me through the glasses. It struck me abruptly that even though he was on his feet, maybe he hadn't intended going yet. But he walked over to me.

"Nice to meet you," he said. "It isn't often I run across such a smart guy."

"Smart?" I put on a grin. "No, you're wrong there. I'm just ordinary people." I'd put on the dumb-Dora act for him, and I was still carrying it through.

"Yes, I can see that." He looked at me then with a funny stare in his eyes. He was breathing in my face again. "Do you know what they do with murderers in the State of California, Stanton?"

"I—"

"They get the gas chamber...."

I said: "W-what?" with the wind going all out of me—but he'd already walked out.

I heard him going down the steps. I stood there looking at the door. I slammed it shut, then I couldn't get my breath. I whirled around to the noise behind me. My face drained white. It was Emmie, opening the bedroom door. I figured she'd heard everything. I began to sweat. Words tumbled out:

"I—I guess you heard—"

She reached over and pressed my hand. "Do you know what I was doing while you were talking to him?"

"What?"

"I refused to listen. I was reading *Better Homes and Gardens*. Oh, I have some wonderful ideas for our house, darling!"

I just looked at her.

13

"The *gas chamber*...."

Judd bothered me plenty. He was the last thing I worried about before I went to sleep and the first thing on my mind the next morning. I got out of bed thinking: could he mean *me?* Was the guy trying to be subtle? Maybe I was imagining things. It was only a statement he'd made—meaning Atkins. Judd had nothing on *me!*

But I still kept thinking about it. Emmie said she had to play for the choir rehearsal. She was on the war bond committee and she said her job was to go from door to door getting people to pledge to buy more bonds. She said after the choir rehearsal she'd be busy all day.

So I stalled around the house till after she left, then I beat it down to see Pop. I figured I'd better stop where he lived first—because he'd told me he wasn't going to open the restaurant again for a few days.

I knew where his house was, because he'd pointed it out once when he drove me to Lilac and Palm in his old jalopy. But I'd never been inside his joint. He lived alone in a little two-room frame building in back of a white stucco. Two houses on one lot—but Pop's quarters looked like a kid's playhouse.

I found the stucco, and hurried down the driveway. At the house in the rear, I rang the bell. I buzzed it a few times and waited. Pop wasn't home. I began hoofing it down to the restaurant.

Pop wasn't serving any customers. He was alone in there. He saw me and came over and opened the door. I got a strong whiff of his whiskey breath. He acted a little strange—like he wasn't any too glad to see me.

We didn't say anything at first. We sat down at the counter, and pretty soon Pop made a feeble gesture toward the back partition.

"I'm goin' to close up this place, Eric. How can I cook there when I can still see her lyin' on the—" His mouth began to twitch.

I said: "Hell, you got dough. You can go somewhere and forget it. You can take that trip you told me about."

"I got to." He held out his hand and showed me how much it was shaking. "I'm no good for nothin'. I wish you could whitewash somethin' like this out of your mind—"

"You take that trip. You sneak away. Don't let those cop bastards bother you—pester you with questions. Listen, Pop—that cop you told me about was over to see me last night."

He blinked up. "I talked to him, too. He walked home with me from the funeral. His name is Mark Judd."

"Yeah." I got a funny feeling then, because I hadn't seen Judd at the funeral. "He told me about the stuff you bought Stella." I was watching Pop carefully. I saw his face redden.

"He *knows* about that, Eric?"

"Hell, yes. He found some sales slips for the perfume. All he had to do was check at the drugstore to find out who'd bought it."

He sniffed and rubbed his nose. "I was hopin' nobody'd find out about that. I only did it 'cause she liked perfume. I liked to do little things for her. She was a good girl. But she always picked the wrong company. She wasn't raised up right, and she didn't know no better. I used to wear out my lungs preachin' to her—but the only time she'd listen to me was when I bought her that kind of perfume she liked."

"And expensive jewelry," I said.

He looked over quick. "I never gave her jewelry."

"Then where'd she get it?"

He shook his head. "I dunno. She never had it until just recently."

"How recent?"

"Month or two mebbe."

I wondered if he was telling the truth. If so, then who did give Stella that jewelry! Where'd she get it! How many others besides Pop were buying her stuff?

"Pop," I said, "she got it somewhere. If you didn't buy it, who did?"

He shook his head again. "I dunno. But let's not talk about her." He held his hand over the region of his heart. "I'm an old man. If I think about it too much, I—"

There was a sudden tapping on the window. I turned and saw

the uniform. It was the cop I'd talked to in the kitchen, when Stella was found dead. Pop went over and unlatched the door. The cop came inside and said:

"You're wanted up at the police station, Mister Elliot."

Pop's jaw dropped. "For what?"

"We got Dave Atkins. Just brought him in. Judd wants you to identify him."

Pop clenched his fist. He picked up his hat from the chair and socked it on his head. "Let's get goin'!" He said it like the Lone Ranger. He marched to the door, then turned back because the cop wasn't beside him.

The cop was still standing by the counter and he was giving me the slow once-over, like he just now saw me for the first time.

"Hello, Mister Stanton," he said good-naturedly. "I was just going up to your house. You saved me the trip. Judd wants you to identify him, too."

"Identify him?" I said. "I'd like to break his neck!" I got up and moved toward the door. "I'll be glad to help any way I can."

The jailhouse was in back of the City Hall. The cop led Pop and me across a small lawn—past the barred window cells. Inside there, you could hear somebody making a hell of a rumpus, banging steel. It sounded to me like it might be the bed. You know how hick town jails are. They have beds that fold up in the wall and a heavy chain that holds them when they're put down. Well, it sounded like somebody was throwing the bed up with all his strength, over and over, into the wall.

The cop led us up some steps, into a stucco building. There was another flat-foot sitting behind the desk just inside. Then we went down a narrow hall and the cop opened a door.

It was dark inside, and at first all I could see was the spotlight. Through the sides of the shadowy figures I glimpsed Atkins seated under the glare. I heard the voice from somewhere. Flat and toneless. I saw the slouched hat: Judd.

Pop felt along the wall and finally found a chair. I followed suit, but our cop escort said: "Not there, Stanton." He took my arm and led me over to another chair by the window. I wondered what difference it made but I sat where the cop said.

From here I had a good view of Atkins. He was licking his lips and blinking up at the light. He was one sorry sight. He had a short stubble of black whiskers with sweat beads shining, and his face was pale behind it. He looked greasy. He didn't look like the handsome walrus. I wished Stella could've seen him with that oily hair rumpled, with that God-fearing stare on his pan. How could she have stood him! I thought.

I could see better now. I could see Judd's figure sitting on the desk right next to the spot. He was talking low to another guy who a cop called "Sheriff." So I figured it was the sheriff who was about ready to grill Atkins. Maybe Judd was trying to give him a little advice. Because it was Judd who was talking and the sheriff was nodding.

I was conscious of the stink of stale, putrid tobacco smoke, and there was still that banging from the jail. I noticed a bouquet of roses on the desk—and that struck my funny bone. Cops with posies on their desks! I couldn't help grinning. My nerves began to relax then and there.

Judd was talking to the sheriff, but you couldn't hear anything he said on account of the din. The noise from the jailhouse was floating through the air—loud. Regularly every half minute you'd hear the crash. It jangled my nerves. You couldn't hear yourself think.

I saw Judd glance at the blacked-out window and make a wry face. He looked over at one of the cops and yelled: "There's a way of quieting that Mex!"

The cop said yes *sir*, sort of happily, and Judd and the sheriff were talking again.

In a few minutes the banging stopped and there was loud Mexican swearing from the jailhouse. I understand Mexican. (Hell, I bummed around in Mexico City for three years when I was a kid.) This guy was yelling that he was no vagrant, like they told him he was. He wanted out. He wanted out *now*. Or he'd kill the whole bunch of cops, he'd break down the jail with his bare fists. He said he was on his way to the San Joaquin Valley to get a job. That was how he happened to be riding the rails. The only reason he came into this town was because he was hungry. He said he never killed anybody in his whole life. It was an insult to even accuse him. Then he was swearing again. The guy really got to the point.

But in the middle of one of the swear words there was a hollow thud. There were two more thuds right in a row—and after that there was no more swearing, no banging, no nothing. Only a sickly silence.

I looked over at the posies again—to make sure I'd seen right. My nerves began shooting up to high C. From the smell of it, they were suspecting the Mexican after all. The guy'd been hanging onto the rails. There was a railroad about a mile out of town. Amigo said he'd come into town because he was hungry ... hungry and looking for food! It was late ... he could have seen the lights on at Pops....

An ache hit my stomach. Jesus! I hoped they didn't wring a confession out of that guy. It was the walrus I wanted to see squirm!

I saw a cop standing beside me. I touched his coat sleeve, and he put his head down.

"Didn't Atkins kill her?" I asked in a low voice.

"I don't know yet," he said. " Judd'll find out—damn quick."

"Judd?" I echoed. "Well—isn't it the sheriff's place to—"

He put his mouth down to my ear. "Listen—when Judd's around everybody stands back. The sheriff wants him to handle everything his own way."

I nodded, but I was tense again. *Judd, Judd, Judd!* This cop talked about him like he was—I caught my breath. I remembered seeing the name. In a *True Detective* magazine—*Mark Judd! The entire story was about him—telling how many murderers he'd sent up!*

I was hollow. I tugged on the cop's sleeve again. He bent down.

"Didn't I see Judd's name in a detective magazine? Is he—"

The cop nodded without letting me finish. "He nails 'em after the rest give up. He's the smartest dick on New York Homicide. And we've got respect for the way he works."

I had the shakes all of a sudden. *I'd thought he was a Walton sheriff or something! I'd thought he was a jerk!*

"Your gun's registered, you say?"

Judd was talking now, addressing Atkins. He was standing with his hands thrust down in his pockets. He was even calmer today. It made me sick just to watch him, he was so calm.

Atkins looked up, but he couldn't see anybody. He kept blinking the light out of his eyes. "Chrissake, yes," he said. "I told you that. I got to have a gun in my business." He looked like he was going to start bawling.

"You say your business is pinball machines? You had a setup in Yuma?"

"Phoenix," Atkins said. "And everything was within the law," he added quickly. "I pack the gun because sometimes I carry a lot of loose cash."

I saw that there was an old guy sitting up at the desk, behind Judd, taking down everything that was said.

Judd said, "All right, baby—tell me your life history. Beginning when you met Stella Flint. I want to know everything that was ever said between you. I don't care if it takes all night."

"I knew her mother," Atkins said. "I used to board at their house in Phoenix."

Something caught in my throat. *This* was the guy Stella told me about the first night I went out with her. The guy who'd had eyes on her, the one she hit over the head with a flower pot. *This* was the reason she left home!

"That was how I knew Stella," he said, "I roomed at the house." His hands were shaking. His face was whiter now. "It was just a room," he went on. "All I got with it was covers, a two buck dresser and a rug." He looked up again, trying to see somebody. "What I mean is, Stella never could see me. It was strictly ice-tea." He coughed. "But she and me and her old lady always ate dinner in the dining room. And I used to sit across the table watching her. I couldn't get my eyes full enough. But she always gave me the cold shoulder. She didn't like me—and it almost drove me nuts."

He gulped and looked around for somebody to say something. Nobody did. The room was quiet and dark, and the stillness screamed through the air. Atkins licked his lips and went on:

"But I guess she felt sorry for me—because one night she let me take her to a movie. After the show I asked her if she wanted a drink and she said no. I knew she drank with the other guys and I asked her if she'd just have one and go home. But it was no soap.

I didn't know what to do. I was all screwed up. Looking at her made me kind of sick, hollow—know what I mean? She was so—"

"Never mind," Judd said. "Did you take her home or didn't you?"

"Not directly. We went up a side street, parked—under a tree. It was dark. She said, 'What's the idea?' I said, 'I just want to talk to you.' She said, 'All right, give me a cigarette.' I did and lit one myself. We sat there and smoked and talked. Only I didn't tell her anything. I was afraid to tell her how I *really* felt."

Judd said: "Skip to where you both finished your cigarettes."

Atkins tried to look at him. "Well—"

"Did you go on the make for her, or didn't you?"

"Well—"

There was a silence. I watched Judd remove something from his pocket. I saw that it was a glove. He jabbed his left hand into it, then slowly began to smooth his fingers into the pigskin. His eyes didn't leave Atkins. Finally he turned down the top of the glove so that it covered his knuckles.

I looked up at the cop beside me. "What the—"

The cop bent down again. "Judd doesn't want to get his knuckles all skinned up."

A cold shiver went through me.

"I warn you," Judd snapped, "we want the truth! You heard what happened to the Mexican. That's nothing at all, mister."

Atkins was staring at the gloved hand. "I tried to kiss her."

"You tried to? You mean you did kiss her!"

"Yes, I did."

"Sure you did! Not once but a couple times—square on the mouth. Wet kisses and you got lipstick—" He was talking fast, breathing hard.

"I—"

"And then your hands got busy—those big paws of yours—and the first thing you know you were—"

Atkins made a leap from the chair. Before I could think, Judd had knocked him back down: the gloved left hand right across Atkins' kisser. I couldn't believe my eyes. Atkins just sat there, sort of stunned, rubbing his mouth with his hand.

Judd's voice came over, calm again:

"Go on from there."

"I—don't—know what you mean." Atkins talked like he had mush in his mouth, but it wasn't mush it was blood.

"Did the rape come off or didn't it?"

"It wasn't rape, it—"

"You know what I'm talking about," Judd rasped.

Atkins nodded. "That—well, no. She—she scratched—" He broke off staring at the blood in his hand. He licked his tongue over his teeth, then got out a handkerchief and spit into it. "She scratched—kicked, everything else. Fine—finally, she got her shoe up and hit me across the head. With the high heel I mean."

He waited again, and still nobody said anything. He drew a deep breath and rubbed one hand over his mouth again. I saw Judd watching him. I saw his eyes glued on him, and I could hear him breathing.

"Go ahead." Judd's voice was crisp now, more nasal.

"She—she'd never go out again with me." He paused, trying to think. "Then I'd have to sit across the table—from her, and she wouldn't speak—except to say pass the butter, things like that." He held his mouth for a moment and went on. "Her—old lady didn't even catch on about Stella and me. I used to go to my room and lie awake nights thinking about her. That's when I made up my mind I had to move. I—had to get away from her! Every night I'd tell myself I had to move! But I didn't. I don't know why I didn't. I kept staying there."

He thought again. "She never spoke, and whenever I—I'd come in the room where she was she'd up and leave." He spit in the handkerchief. "She wouldn't—talk to me anymore. It was driving me nuts! I wanted to hur—hurt her. If there was only some way I could hurt her—"

Judd's voice shot through the air. "Say it, Atkins—make it easy on yourself. Get it off your chest. You wanted to *kill* her. Say it!"

The walrus cringed. "No, I never wanted to kill her!"

"You didn't want to—*but you did!*" Judd was beside him again.

"I—I tell you I—didn't."

I heard the crunch of bone. Judd let him have it again. He put all his strength in that left-handed wallop. Atkins looked up bewildered, stunned, wondering what in the hell hit him. Then he was spitting out blood again. But this time his face got red.

Veins stood out on his forehead.

"*You dirty son-of-a-bitch!*" he shouted. "I don't know who you are but you'll pay for this!"

Judd was back at him. He brought the gloved hand down fast, and when it came up he got the walrus again. Atkins shook his head like he was dazed.

Blood drummed sickeningly in my ears. A dumb, Walton cop! Jesus! This guy was dynamite!

Judd said: "Go on. We want the rest of it."

Atkins was whimpering. He looked up, his face ashen. His nose was bleeding now. I looked up at the cop beside me and he looked down at me.

Then Atkins was talking again. It was nauseating watching him. He couldn't get the words out, his lips were swollen and beginning to turn blue. I could only catch some of the words:

"It got so—my pinball machines—I didn't care—how they were doing. I—hung around the house—"

"Speak up!" Judd told him.

He spoke up. "I was—hoping her mother'd leave—so I could talk. When we were alone she'd talk to me. Something—nasty, but she'd say something—and that was all that mattered. One day her mother was—gone—I made up my mind. I found her in—in the front room. I grabbed her and—next thing I knew she'd—reached for the flower pot—somewhere on the mantel. I woke up an hour later. She wasn't there. Then I—I had to tell the old lady about it. She was sore. We—we got the cops—started looking for Stella—put ads in the paper—everything. Then afterwards it was all right; her—old lady settled down—just sort of gave up."

He wiped his nose with the bloody handkerchief and thought for a minute. "I don't know why I didn't move then. I waited for her to come back. I—waited six months, kept hounding the—mailman." His eyes came up. "I thought maybe she'd gone—to Hollywood. She talked about it sometimes—getting in pictures. Or maybe she was working as a show girl somewhere. But finally—her mother got the postcard. Walton, California. I came here—"

His voice grew bitter. "I found her—in a greasy little restaurant. She was a—waitress."

"We know the rest," Judd said. "You bought your way in with jewelry—watches and stuff."

"I never bought her anything."

Judd ignored him. "You got her out with you and tried your tactics all over again."

Atkins blinked up. "I only wanted to talk to her."

Judd smiled sarcastically. "I suppose that was how you ripped her dress—trying to *talk* to her?"

Atkins steeled himself in the chair. You could tell he was seething inside.

"She—fell. That's how she ripped—her dress."

"*I'm* telling this, Atkins. You took her out. You left the Blue Lantern Café at nine-thirty. You took her other places. Where?"

"Nowhere else. We—stopped along the beach—to talk."

"To *argue*, don't you mean?"

"Well, I was trying to get her to go home—back to Arizona. Her mother—But it was no use. I knew I'd have to go back alone."

"You started to go back alone," Judd snapped. "Then you came back. What was it you told her when you got out of your car and came back?"

"I—don't know what you mean. I let her out in front."

"Listen, Atkins—the landlady saw you stop the car and go back."

"I didn't—I kept driving."

"You're lying! What ruse did you pull to get her to take you in the restaurant?"

Atkins looked up. Suddenly he was blinking back the tears. "That—was where she was *killed*, wasn't it?"

Judd cackled a laugh. "Suppose you tell *me!*"

The walrus stared mutely. "I—left her out in front—where she lived."

Judd was beside him again. "No, you didn't. You got her in Pop's place somehow. It was all premeditated, wasn't it? You knew exactly what you were going to do!" He was breathing down in Atkins' face. "What'd you kill her with? A piece of iron pipe? *Did you hit her with a pipe?*"

Atkins was on his feet. "I *didn't!*" he shouted. "I tell you I didn't!"

Judd motioned to the cops. "Lock him up," he said calmly.

The drapes swished open. Light from outside rushed in. I saw they'd given Atkins bracelets. Two cops led him out. Judd glanced at me once. Then he was all excited, talking to the sheriff. I saw that Pop was on his feet, going over to them. I got up quick and cut in ahead of Pop.

"You want to see me, Mister Judd?"

He turned from the sheriff. His myopic eyes squinted at me. "Yes." He gave me the slow once-over. "You said you saw Stella Flint at 8 P.M. on the night of September 28 getting into a Buick coupe in front of Pop's place?"

"Yeah."

"Was Dave Atkins the man in the Buick?"

"It was him all right."

He nodded. "Okay. You can go."

I beat it outside quick. Then all of a sudden I was weak again.

I remember later that night. Emmie and I were at the dinner table. We heard somebody shouting the extra:

Killer Captured!

I ran down the steps. People were gathered out in front of the grocery store—everybody shouting and talking. I got a weekly paper from the news kid and went back upstairs. Emmie and I read Atkins' story together. Cops or the editor had soft-pedaled it, because it was milk and water stuff.

There was a picture of him too, slumped down on the bed in his cell. One of his eyes was black and blue, puffed to a slit. It made me sick to my stomach: they'd grilled him again.

But I guess the town of Walton slept peacefully that night.

14

The next morning I knew it was high time to scram. Atkins was being held. Atkins was making his way toward San Quentin. My thoughts were back on the pork barrel—the time was now. The first step was to find a house. Emmie was willing to spend her bond money to buy it, and that was all that was necessary.

So we began the search. Emmie took me to see a realtor. He was an Irishman, named Maloney. He drove us in his car, a shiny blue Ford sedan, hauled us all around. He'd known Emmie's father and the two of them found a lot to gab about.

He showed us four houses, inside and out. Emmie found fault with them all. If the kitchen was handy, the back lawn space was too small. If the house wasn't too old, the closet space was too dinky. If the back lawn was big enough, the front windows didn't look out to the street. I got plenty irritated that first day.

The next two days we took the Plymouth. We looked at more houses. There was one for sale two miles out of Walton. It faced the ocean. It was back on a hill, a Spanish house with a side patio and umbrellas. The owner lived there—a Swede with an accent. He showed us all through and gave us a drink of red wine and told us the price: fourteen thousand bucks. He said it had a six-thousand-dollar mortgage. It required eight thousand down and payments of seventy-five dollars a month.

Back in the Plymouth, Emmie said there was no use of us even thinking about it, because it was more than we could afford. So we continued the hunt.

On the fourth day, just before we were starting out again, the grocer downstairs came up and said I was wanted on the phone.

It was Maloney. He said I have just the place you're looking for, Mister Stanton. It's only seventy-seven seventy-five, the lot is fifty by a hundred and fifty. It's a little dream—just what the Missus wants. Seventy-seven seventy-five. That includes everything. The owner pays escrow, the title and everything. I took down the address and said I'll meet you there in ten minutes.

Emmie agreed with Maloney that the house was a little dream.

The owner—Maloney told us—was living in the East and the place was empty. We all walked through it five times. Maloney said it was the best buy he'd ever seen. He said he'd been put in charge of disposing of it, so we'd better close the deal right now because there were a lot of other people interested.

Emmie opened cupboard and closet doors and kitchen drawers. She tried the faucets for some reason or other, and measured floor spaces by pacing back and forth across the rooms. She decided that the back porch was big enough, and though the back lawn space wasn't half what she wanted, it would do. She asked me didn't I like it, and I said I did and Maloney began rubbing his hands.

After all, she said, there was a war being fought, and people couldn't be too particular.

She said we'd better go right to Mister Maloney's office and give him a deposit. It took some fast talking on my part, and Maloney's face sagged when I began gumming the works.

"Let's not be too hasty, Emmie," I said. "Let's think it over tonight. If we still want the place by tomorrow, that's time enough."

She said that I was being perfectly sensible. I got in the Plymouth and started the motor and she said good-bye to Maloney and told him she'd get in touch with him in the morning.

You see, the day after we came back on our honeymoon, Emmie notified the bank about cashing in her bonds. I knew they'd already sent her a check for the full amount and she'd deposited it in her checking account. I also knew that I had to do this thing cleverly. No bungling. I wanted to do it in a way that kept the law off my neck. I'd already planned the way to work it, and right now was the minute for some fast maneuvering.

I saw a clock. Two-thirty. I drove straight toward the bank.

"Emmie," I said, "you're sure that's the house you want?"

"Darling, in spite of its bad points, I think it will be quite comfortable."

"It's yours then. And I'll tell you what I'll do. You pay for it, and as soon as I can get my dough I'll give it all back to you. Every penny."

She smiled. "I'll put it right back in war bonds."

"Oh, sure. We got to be patriotic."

I had my next speech all figured out:

"Listen carefully, Emmie. That house isn't worth the price they're asking. Believe me, I know values. Now Maloney is getting about three hundred bucks from the owner to sell it. That's his commission. But I know how to handle those birds. Tomorrow morning I'll get him alone in his office and give *him* a sales talk. I'll get him to split his commission. That is, we'll get the house for a hundred and fifty less than he's asking. It isn't fair for him to gyp us like that."

She was looking at me and nodding, then she said: "But dear, I've known Frank Maloney for years and years. I'm sure he wouldn't take unfair advantage of—"

"Listen, Emmie, I don't trust any realtor. I'm going to get that house cheaper. Hell, he expects to have to come down."

I was saying all this to throw her off. I was ready to shoot the fireworks. I went on casually:

"So we'll drop past the bank and have them fix up a joint account, so's I can do business with Maloney. And don't you see, I don't want him to think *you're* buying the house with your dough. It doesn't look good."

She reached over and kissed my cheek. "Of course, darling. I never thought of it that way."

I pulled up in front of the bank. We went inside, and Emmie talked to the teller for a few minutes. Pretty soon a little guy brought some papers for me to sign. My hand was shaking, but I got my signature down just fine.

Back in the Plymouth, Emmie said:

"Well, it's done, darling. We'll buy the little house tomorrow then...."

Tomorrow then ... It kept grinding through my brain—like a needle stuck in a phonograph record! *Tomorrow then*—I'd get the dough! I'd be at the bank the first thing in the morning. Then I'd start moving. Anywhere. I'd keep on the move. *Tomorrow then*.... I'd begin life all over. I'd have myself one hell of a sweet time!

I put the car in the garage, facing Lilac Street. Emmie and I walked around the corner, on Palm, past the grocery shop and started up the steps.

"Oh, hello, Mister Stanton...."

It was the same cop that took Pop and me to the jailhouse. He was standing at the bottom of the stairs, looking up. He'd probably been waiting for me to come home.

"Judd wants to see you," he said. "Down at the station."

15

The cop drove me in his car, back down through town. We walked past the jailhouse again, and up the steps. We went down the corridor and he opened a door to his right.

Judd was inside there, standing behind a desk. At the sight of him my heart sank. The cop led me inside, then went out and closed the door.

It was an ordinary office and very stuffy, with a tan rug and two floor lamps. All the electric lights were on, though it was broad daylight. Thick curtains hung over a door in the rear, and I supposed a private washroom was back there.

Judd looked up and saw me. The lines around his mouth gave him a haggard expression. His lips were twisted in thought. "Sit down, Stanton." He said this looking down at the newspaper on his desk. He kept sucking in the foul air.

I dropped down in a chair before the desk. I heard him rustling the paper, traffic from Main Street. I heard my heart thumping in my ears. It was quite a while before Judd's eyes came up—gleaming behind the glasses.

I said: "What's on your mind, Mister Judd?"

He rubbed his nose with his thumb. "I've been over talking to your wife's sister. She's a pretty sick woman."

"In the head," I said. It took all my strength to sit there acting casual. "Clara's off the beam. You'd be wise not to take stock in anything she says. I think she's real dangerous."

"Crazy you say?"

I nodded. "It'd be doing the community a favor if somebody reserved her a room in the bughouse."

Judd's face was expressionless. "As far as that goes, the nut galleries would be full if everybody was put there who belonged."

I didn't think it was funny, but I grunted a laugh. I wanted to get along with this guy.

He was eying me again. "Atkins didn't kill Stella Flint," he said quietly. "I'm letting him go. I—" His voice died out. He went over to the window and stood peering down.

I didn't know whether I'd heard him right. I said, "You say Atkins didn't kill her?"

"Atkins proved he bought gas at a service station in Fulton—at two in the morning the night Stella was killed. Fulton is a hundred miles from here." He paused. "The autopsy proved she was killed *after* two o'clock. It was closer to four in the morning."

Something caught in my throat. "But the paper said they found his fingerprints in the kitchen. It said—"

"Papers?" He crossed back to his desk and slumped down in the swivel chair and put his legs up on the desk. "I tell them bedtime stories. The only prints we found belonged to the waitress and Ben Elliot." He lit a cigarette. "As far as Atkins goes, I couldn't have pinned it on him if I'd wanted to." He was leering at me again. "Somebody confronted Stella Flint *after* she left Atkins—and just *before* she reached the rooming house steps. Somebody was waiting for her there in the shadows of the house. Whoever it was killed her. That's my hunch."

A shiver went through me. There was a long silence while Judd breathed heavily.

"Wasn't there some sort of a pact between you and the girl?" he asked abruptly.

"Pact?" I got goose-pimples. He'd caught me unawares. "I don't know what you're talking about!"

He gave me a sloppy smile. "Like you were going to get some dough and take her away?"

"Dough? Take her away?" My knees felt like they were turning to water. "Hell, no, Mister Judd. Where'd you get that idea?"

"I get a lot of ideas," he said. "You weren't jealous of her or Atkins?"

"Hell, no!"

"You didn't threaten her life?" he asked calmly.

"You got your wires crossed, mister, you got the wrong number."

The smile was still on his lips. "I don't think so. Ben Elliot told me he was resting on a cot in the kitchen one day and he heard you tell Stella that if she went out with somebody else you'd break her head." His voice was loud suddenly, nasal. "Well—*you did it, didn't you?*"

"Pop ought to clean out the wax! I said I'd break *his* head!

Atkins' head!"

He whirled on me. "*Then you were jealous of them both!*"

"Jealous?" I was sweating. "Hell, you know how it is, Mister Judd. I was only talking big."

He sprang up from the chair. Then he was strutting around the room. "Talk big *now*, Stanton! Tell *me* what a bigshot you are!" He turned on me again. "I've got a hunch it was you who was waiting for the girl in the shadows of the rooming house!"

I couldn't swallow. "Christ, no!"

"And she said, '*What do you want?*' Remember?"

"No. Christ, no!"

"You didn't meet her in the restaurant either, did you, Stanton?" He was close to me, shouting into my face. "You didn't ask her if she was still going away with you after you'd succeeded in getting some dough! You didn't get hotheaded and kill her because she said she'd changed her mind, *did you?*"

"I—I don't know where you get those ideas," I blurted. "I'm a married man, I'm—"

He cackled a laugh. It put a chill through me. "You can go," he said.

I didn't think I'd heard right. "Did—you say for me to—go?"

He nodded. "Only I wouldn't make any plans to leave this immediate vicinity if I were you—"

"What do you mean?" My voice was too high.

His head came up. "Then you *were* planning on leaving?"

"No, Mister Judd. Of course not."

"Well, what are you worrying about then! Just be on tap, that's all. I may want you." He chuckled humorlessly from his throat. "I'm beginning to like your company."

I laughed, but it was weak. I didn't know what to say.

"Be seeing you," Judd said. His voice was flat. He turned and left the room.

I sat there, motionless, for a long time. Then I got up and went out the door. Outside, I began to swear. It didn't grip me until then. You know damn well what it was. Fear. My feelings were numb until now, but suddenly a wire had snapped inside me. I was weak in the knees, and yet I wanted to run. I wanted to get the hell out and hide. Where? Any place where this nightmare

Nero Wolfe couldn't find me! To the ends of the earth maybe!

I hurried on down the street, my mind a tumult of fear.

Judd was after me all right. Hounding me. Piecing things together. He had only a hunch. A hunch that I killed her! His goddam hunches!

You can't convict a man on hunches! What was I worrying about!

What the hell are you worrying about! Calm down! For Christ's sake, calm down! You've got to stand still with a snake. If you don't he'll strike! Calm down. You're as smart as he is. What you going to do now—botch things up? Let this Judd scare you? That's his scheme—to scare you. He wouldn't have *told* you he suspected you if he didn't have some kind of a scheme. So you're going to let him scare you out right now? Before tomorrow? You've got the biggest thing in your life in the palm of your hands, namely ten thousand bucks, if you'll only stick it out until tomorrow morning! Get that dough!

I was at Lilac and Palm. I passed the grocery store and hurried up the steps. I was turning the key in the lock when I heard her. Clara. Staring at me with hostile eyes and marching up the stairs behind me.

16

She wore a drab green dress that was too long for her as usual and too baggy around the hips. Her shoes were brown oxfords and there was a big flouncy beret on one side of her head. A brown purse hung from a strap off her shoulder. She reminded me of something out of *Vogue* ... 1909.

She gave me the cool hello. I held the door open for her and she hurried on inside. She stuck her pale face close to Emmie and gave her a peck on the cheek. Emmie said:

"I'm so glad to see you, dear."

Clara smiled self-pityingly. "It's good to see you, Emmie."

This was the first time Clara'd been over, so Emmie showed her through the apartment, all the time telling her about the new house we were buying.

I was sitting in the front room, trying to pull myself together. A cold sweat had come over me. My hands were ice cold—and clammy. I knew I had to stick the night out—and that would be the last. No more humoring Emmie, no more run-ins with Judd, no more sessions at the jailhouse. I'd hop a freighter—take the rails out in the morning, after I'd been to the bank, of course.

I thought about all that, but still I was half-listening to the sister act in the kitchen.

Suddenly they were quiet and you could hear low whispering. Then regularly every half minute Clara would come up with something audible. You know how it is when you're trying to tell somebody something private, but for the benefit of somebody who might be listening in the next room, you raise your voice and say something inconsequential? Well, Clara was saying that the curtains in there should be blue instead of yellow—to match the linoleum. Then I heard the whispers again. After that, Clara repeated the same thing she'd said about the curtains.

I got up. Silently I walked across the carpet. At the kitchen doorway, I peered inside. Sure enough their heads were together. Clara was doing the whispering, her eyes wild and glassy, her lips working overtime.

I let them have it:

"You girls got secrets?"

Emmie whirled around and tried to say something and couldn't; and Clara looked like she'd been caught in the strawberry jam. I knew Clara'd been giving Emmie the low-down on what she and Judd had talked about, but I pretended to be disinterested.

"I can leave the house," I went on, "so you girls can talk all you want—"

Emmie came over to me and locked her arm in mine. "You'll do nothing of the sort, Eric. I want Clara to tell you what she's told me. Awful things. Tell him, Clara."

Clara's eyes snapped. "I haven't told you *half*. I haven't told you what a horrible—" She groped for the word. "—*gigolo* you've married."

I managed a grin. Emmie was beside me, puffing with indignation.

"Clara, you will avoid voicing your opinion—"

Clara grunted almost inaudibly. "There isn't an opinion bad enough for him. Why he's the worst—"

"If you can't treat Eric with more respect I must ask you to leave."

"Respect?" Clara came closer, staring vacantly. "You ask me to respect a man whom the Los Angeles police ran out of town? Respect? A man who's swindled and cheated, a man who—"

I felt the blood rushing to my cheeks. The ten grand was suddenly sprouting wings! I knew I had to work fast. If Emmie believed her, I was sunk. It didn't matter what Emmie believed tomorrow after I'd blown, but tonight it meant everything. I had to keep levelheaded. I said calmly:

"I suspect you've been talking to a Mister Judd—"

Clara's head flung up. "Oh, yes—you're quite right. But you have no idea what Mister *Judd* suspects—"

"And what does Mister Judd suspect?" I was mocking her, in the same asinine voice.

Her eyes flashed to Emmie, then back to me. She took a deep breath to bolster her courage. "He told me he has a witness who saw you the night Stella Flint was murdered. You were walking toward her rooming house at midnight." Her eyes got big and scared.

Emmie began to sob. "Oh, Eric—*why* is he doing this to you! You didn't go near that rooming house, did you? Did you, Eric?"

"Of course not."

I heard Clara's voice through my words: "He told me that Eric would be under arrest within twenty-four hours."

"But they've *got* the murderer," Emmie said frantically.

"I'm afraid they haven't," Clara said.

I heard their voices, but it was as though I wasn't there. I was off some place. I was sitting in a theatre maybe, watching stage performers. I was listening in on a radio program. This wasn't real; it was some kind of a drama. But then I knew I was there all right. I heard Clara's heavy breathing, I heard the moan from Emmie's throat through the silence—the steady drip of the sink faucet, the ocean drumming a weird symphony of undertones in the distance. I heard Clara saying:

"I'll help you pack your things."

"Pack? For what?"

"You're leaving him this instant!"

"Really, Clara—"

"You're *not* coming home—when you know what a monstrous beast he is?"

"I asked you to leave. Now I must order you to go. Don't come back until you're prepared to apologize to Eric."

"Emmie, he—he might kill *you*—"

"Clara, stop this at once!"

"He will. Look at him! Look at his eyes. He killed that waitress—and he'll kill you!"

"Oh, Clara—" Emmie's voice was despair.

"I know the *type!* Look at him now. There's no feeling there. He's cold as stone.... Look at the way he's sitting there—just staring straight ahead. He's a madman!"

"*Clara, leave at once!*"

"Do you think I can leave you here? At his mercy? Do you think I can rest one minute knowing you're here *alone* with him! Emmie, *listen* to me. You must listen. I know what I'm saying. He'll kill you—just like he killed *her!* Where are the police? Oh, why don't the police come and take him away!"

Emmie came over to me then. She put one arm down around my shoulders. I reached up and patted her hand. I heard Clara sobbing, only it was more like an animal whine, low in her throat. I saw her body slumped against the wall.

"Come home with me, Emmie. The house is so—lonely. I won't ever be able to sleep if you don't come home. I know he'll kill you. I'm sure of it. I'm afraid for you. I'm afraid the airplanes will hit the house sometimes. I won't be able to sleep anymore. He might come over and murder *me in my sleep!*"

I felt Emmie's hand tightening. She turned abruptly and went over to Clara. The next thing I knew they were in each other's arms. Emmie had tears in her eyes.

"Clara—you poor dear—you're awfully ill, aren't you? I'm sorry. Forgive me. I forgot for a moment how ill you are—"

"Yes. My head—it hurts so much now, I—he'll kill you—"

Emmie looked over at me with a hopeless expression. "Yes, yes, dear, I know. But my place is with my husband. You see, he didn't hurt that waitress. Someone else did."

"He didn't?"

"No, dear."

"Even if he didn't, Emmie—he's still no good. He's a crook. The only reason he married you was to get your money."

"Yes, dear—I know. But I love him very much."

"You shouldn't. If you'd only seen the way he kissed that girl, you'd know you shouldn't."

"Don't think about it. You must think about getting out and meeting people. You mustn't stay alone in the house. Tomorrow I'm going to church and arrange for you to meet some nice new friends."

"Then you'll come home?"

"Oh, yes. Now I'll walk with you down the steps—you mustn't think about anything."

I watched them go out the door. I heard two pair of footsteps walking down, then one walking back up. Emmie was beside me suddenly, wiping the tears from her eyes.

"Something has to be done about her." Her voice was strained and low.

"Yeah."

"I—I'm afraid it's true what—you said she was." She was in my arms then, sobbing on my shoulder. "I didn't realize she was so sick! Something *has* to be done. Tell me, Eric, what to do!"

It was too late now to tell her, too late to work on the bughouse angle, or I'd sold her a final bill of goods. I was busy thinking about what Judd told Clara ... a witness who'd seen me walking toward the rooming house ... twenty-four hours! *I had to have dough now! It took dough to get where cops couldn't find you!*

"And then that horrible Mister Judd! Oh, everything's going to pieces!"

I said: "I don't think he told Clara anything. I guess she's at the stage where they start making up things."

She bit her lip. "She has to have help, poor dear."

"Yeah. She sure does."

She was still sobbing against my shoulder. "Then there wasn't any truth in what she said—that you were asked to leave Los Angeles?"

"Not in the slightest."

"You don't think Judd was to see her at all?"

"Maybe. Maybe he was. I'm not afraid of him." I said that, but I had to let go of her and sit down. My legs were so weak they wouldn't hold me up. "So what has Judd got on me?" I continued slowly. "Nothing at all. He's only got a scheme, Emmie. I don't know what the hell it is. If he *did* have anything on me, he'd arrest me right now. That would make sense! But his plan doesn't make sense! He wouldn't be telling Clara what he was going to do, except for a reason. He knew Clara'd tell you, you'd tell me. He's trying to scare me, maybe. Maybe that's his scheme. To scare me. I guess he figures if I run out that'll prove my guilt somehow."

My voice hardened: "To hell with him! And don't you worry, Emmie. We'll buy that house tomorrow. I'm going to set the alarm and go see the realtor early in the morning. If you say so—we'll even let Clara live with us. I'm a good guy!"

Her face lighted. "Oh, darling, that would solve everything! Poor Clara, she'd—she'd *love* it!" Then she was laughing and crying and kissing me again.

I said: "We've got to eat dinner now and go to bed early. We've got to sleep and forget Judd and Clara and every other goddam thing in the world. Because tomorrow is another day. Tomorrow it will all be different...."

I said that, but when I looked in a mirror I saw the sweat standing out on my forehead in fat, flat blisters.

Tomorrow then ... tomorrow then ... tomorrow then ... tomorrow then.... The needle was stuck in my brain. *Somebody stop that goddam needle!*

In the middle of that night I woke up with a start. I was wide awake, the rumble of the ocean tight in my ears. I stared at the ceiling, feeling suffocated, hollow. My lungs ached. I saw Emmie beside me, breathing heavily, sound asleep.

I got up out of bed. I crept into the front room. It was two or three o'clock. In seven hours the bank would be open. I went over to the window and looked out, I don't know why. Across the dark stretch, a searchlight was combing the ocean. A bright glare of white over the palm trees. I breathed in the raw air.

And then suddenly my blood froze.

There was a tiny flicker of light from the street. It was moving! It moved up to a man's lips! It was the burning coals of a cigarette. I could distinguish the silhouette, the figure, the slouched hat ... *Judd!*

My heart beat an odd, uneven tempo.

I saw his faint movements. He was leaning against a tree, looking up—watching the apartment. I stood there motionless in the dark room. A nauseating wave caught me.

He'd set his trap, and he was waiting for the catch.

It hit me suddenly that he was *expecting* me to make a move tonight. That was part of his plan. Then it was a plan, I was right! The only reason he'd let me go tonight was so he could watch me, see what I'd do—otherwise he'd have locked me up at once—like he did Atkins. But he let me go; it was part of a plan all right.

If I left that alone would prove my guilt. He'd know his hunch was right. But he'd be ready for me; he had no intentions of letting me get away. He was waiting now for the catch! Maybe there were other cops—planted in back—

I caught my breath.

He was sure I'd killed Stella—yet he hadn't arrested me. But how long would he play this game! Only for tonight maybe. By daylight he'd be disgusted, tired from no sleep, sore because I hadn't played into his hands. The trap would still be empty.

Maybe he'd arrest me then, figuring he'd make the kill under a third degree....

A siren screamed through my brain: *Get the hell out! Once Judd sinks his fangs it's too late!*

The *dough!* Christ! My stomach burned. Leaving now meant leaving the dough! Ten thousand bucks, gone up in smoke! But this was the zero hour....

I had the advantage. Judd didn't know I saw him. Luckily, I hadn't turned on a light.

I groped my way back across the room. Moonlight streaked the rug. I found the front room closet, and pulled down a suitcase, Emmie's suitcase, I'd take only a few things. Cops or no cops, I'd get out. I'd get past them. I'd head for the railroad tracks. What was I doing with the suitcase—excess baggage. Suddenly I whirled around to the sound at my left. I was shaking from head to foot.

"Eric—what in the world...."

My stomach began to turn over.

Emmie was standing in the bedroom doorway, rubbing the cold from her shoulders. Abruptly her eyes were on the suitcase. My heart stopped for a moment.

"Where you going?"

I got up and motioned for her to be quiet. I took her hand and led her over to the window. I pointed down and she saw the shadowy figure. Her eyes came up slowly.

"Who is it?"

"Judd."

She looked at me in swift bewilderment. "What does he want?"

"I don't know," I whispered numbly. "Maybe there's more cops."

"Why?" she asked tensely.

"Christ, I don't know. But I'm not waiting to find out. I'm ducking out."

When she breathed normally again she said: "You were—going away—without telling me?"

"You think I'm that kind of a louse?"

"Don't get excited, dear." Her voice was trembling again. "I don't understand it at all. They have the murderer and yet—"

"Atkins didn't do it," I said. "They're letting him go." I saw her startled expression through the darkness.

"They actually think *you*—"

I nodded. "Circumstances are against me. But circumstances can easily convict me. I've known several guys railroaded—just as innocent as I am."

Her eyes widened. "I've heard of that. They always convict somebody—"

"Yeah. Judd's a New York cop. He never gives up. Hell, he couldn't afford not to fry me. It'd ruin his reputation if he couldn't solve this murder." I looked at her. "I know the way they work."

She had one hand on my arm and her fingernails dug my flesh. "Yes, you must go where you'll be safe. I'm afraid something awful's up. I'll hurry and get dressed—"

"For what?"

"I'm going with you, dear."

"Emmie, you can't! You—"

She put her fingers on my lips. "I must go with you. I can't stay here and wonder where you are, whether you're safe. I must go, darling!" She started to cry again. "Please—please, let me go. Don't leave me here. I—"

"Shh— Be quiet."

She was in my arms, holding me with all her strength. "Please, please, please, darling, take me with you!"

I stared at her. Things were in enough turmoil without a weeping dame on my hands. What would she pull next! I was suddenly fed up to the teeth. She was hanging on to me for dear life, her head buried in my chest, sobbing noiselessly. Leave it to a dame to fold up at a crucial moment, I thought.

My head was all agony. The dough was thrown overboard, Emmie was going to louse everything if she—Then something snapped inside me. Why *not* take her with me? Why hadn't I thought of it before! A moment ago I'd kissed the ten grand good-bye. We had a joint account; I could draw out the dough from the Walton bank, but in another town I'd never get by cashing a check in the thousands. But here was the angle—with Emmie *with* me, with it being *her* dough, she could get the check cashed all right. Why not take her as far as Frisco, and—

"We'll take the Plymouth," she said.

I kept looking at her. "We can't get it out of the garage. The cops'll hear the motor, they'll—"

"We can push it," she whispered. "We can push it down two blocks before we start the motor."

"Yeah. But if there's cops in back—"

Her eyes lighted. "The stairway, Eric—*the closet stairway!* It leads down to the grocery store." She was talking fast. "We can go out the side door on Lilac Street. Even if the police are watching the back steps, we'll be out of their sight."

I felt as though someone had jabbed me with a pin. "Okay, Emmie—let's get on our clothes—fast!"

I went down the stairs first, Emmie close behind me. I felt the cobwebs on my face. Our feet hit the cement, then we were moving past boxes and counters in the grocery store. We reached the side door.

The key was in the lock. I turned it without making a sound. Still the door wouldn't open. I saw a night latch three feet up. I unlatched it and turned the knob. The door creaked open.

A cold breeze hit my lungs. There was no one on the sidewalk. There was only the throb of the ocean, growing loud and soft and loud again, the gray blanket of night. We hurried through the shadows of the buildings.

The garages were just this side of the alley, not in the alley, but facing Lilac Street. Emmie turned a key in the lock and slid the latch over. I jerked the door up. It was the kind that slid up and rested on the roof of the garage.

I motioned for Emmie to get in the car. She did, and released the brake. I gave one hard push and the Plymouth was rolling back down the runway. I pulled the garage door back down and fastened the lock. I was in the street then. Emmie had the wheels turned. I gave another push and kept pushing.

About a block and a half down, I jumped in the driver's seat and started the motor. We were rolling. Through the mirror I glimpsed dimmed headlights. Blood hummed in my ears. I stepped on the gas.

"It's only a milk truck," Emmie said.

A few minutes later we were on the highway. I turned the headlights on full and began burning the pavement.

"Where we going?" Emmie's voice sounded far away.

"Frisco. If we get that far. It depends on Judd. If his plan is to arrest me tonight, we're sunk. There'll be cop cars in the next town, ready to pick us up. But if he's only watching the house we got a chance. Maybe he won't discover we've gone until tomorrow."

I thought of Judd, standing there in the cold—waiting. Well, you bastard, I thought, here's hoping you have a long wait!

I drove on, and neither of us said anything. Emmie was sitting close to me, with her eyes on the road. She was a pretty smart little dame after all, I thought. She'd used her head in getting me out. I put my hand under her chin and pulled her over and kissed her.

I said: "That's for using your head, baby."

She snuggled up in her coat and smiled at me. Then her teeth began to chatter. I was conscious suddenly that mine were too.

17

It was daylight outside, and my eyes were burning, fingers cramped. The sun had been up maybe two hours. We were entering another town. There was a department store to our right. Sears Roebuck. It covered a whole block. I saw a sign: Free Parking In Rear.

I turned in at the alley and parked in the lot. In a couple hours the store would open and the space would be jammed. Cops wouldn't think of looking back there; they'd be watching the highways. I explained to Emmie that it was time to abandon the Plymouth: license plates were too easily traced. We got out of the car. Frisco was about a hundred and fifty miles yet.

We walked back to the street. I saw an open café. We went in and had breakfast. I asked the waitress what time the Frisco Greyhound came through. She went in the back and asked the cook and came back outside and said two-twenty this afternoon.

"We can't wait for it," I told Emmie. "We got to walk back to where the two highways crossed. It's about a mile. We'll thumb a ride."

"You mean we'll—hitchhike?"

"Yeah."

"You mean—we have to stand along the road and hold out our hands?"

"I'll do the thumbing," I said irritably.

She gave me a strange look.

We finished our coffee, then we were outside again, hoofing it down the highway. I saw that her nose was beet red from the cold, and I kidded her about that. She pulled her wool scarf tight around her head and tied it under her chin. She said she was glad she'd worn warm clothes. She had on a black wool suit with sort of a white tie at the neck, and a top coat thrown over her shoulders.

We'd gone maybe eight blocks when a truck stopped. The driver was a pale-faced kid. He asked us if we wanted a ride. I said "sure, kid," and Emmie and I hopped in beside him. The truck started out again.

"On your way to work?" the kid asked.

I said yeah. It was about seven o'clock—the time guys went to work.

"At the airplane factory?"

I nodded. I didn't know there was an airplane factory around there, but I had to steer the guy off. If Judd knew we were gone he'd sent out a general alarm by now—our descriptions.

I said: "My sister and I both work at the factory."

We were approaching the crossroads now.

"Let us off here, bud," I said.

"Aw, I'll take you folks right on down to the factory. It ain't much out of my road."

"Never mind, kid. We always catch a ride here with a buddy of mine."

He pulled to a stop and told us he was glad to help us out. The truck turned to the left, and Emmie said:

"You think fast. I wouldn't have known what to tell him."

I laughed. "My mind works that way, sis."

We crossed the highway and waited. There was a boulevard stop sign there, so I knew we wouldn't have a long wait. A school bus passed, filled with kids. A couple more cars passed. I gave them the thumb, but they kept right on going, most of them not even bothering to stop.

But finally a blue coupe rolled up. The guy inside stuck his head out and looked up at the road signs. It gave the names of all the nearby towns, with arrows pointing. I nailed him.

"Going to Frisco, mister?"

He looked at me, then at Emmie. "About forty miles this side. Sure, hop in."

He turned out to be a brassiere salesman. He told us his name and how good business was, even though, he said, they couldn't get nylon or elastic anymore.

I half listened to him. I was still shaky. Up till now I hadn't had much time to think. But jogging along the road, I began to wonder about the Mexican they were holding in the jailhouse. Why in the hell couldn't they make him confess and get the whole thing over.

Or why didn't they pick up Pop? But then, it wasn't too logical—that they'd really suspect an old man like that.

Why didn't Judd get a hunch that Clara killed her? To protect Emmie's interests could be her motive. Hell, yes—she saw me with Stella that night, and she could have made up her mind to bump off the competition for her sister. A crazy woman can muster a lot of strength!

Why weren't they rounding up the bus driver Stella'd gone off with—or even Madley? Yeah. Why didn't Judd dream up a case against Madley?

Why pick on *me*? And what did Judd mean asking if there was a pact between Stella and me! Where was he getting his information? From Pop—maybe. Maybe Stella had let Pop in on everything.

I thought about all this while we drove on, even while we stopped for lunch at a roadside café. The salesman was doing all the talking, but I finally got in that Emmie was my sister. Constance, I called her, to throw this guy off. I told him we lived in Frisco, we'd been visiting an uncle in the country and buses were so crowded we'd decided to hitchhike back

The guy paid for our lunch and, outside again, took a black suitcase from the back of his car. He gave Emmie a brassiere and told her there was no bra in the world like a Snuggie Whirlpool.

Late that afternoon he said he had to turn off and go into San Jacinto. So Emmie and I got out and thanked him, and he was on his way.

We were away from the ocean now. There were little farmhouses on either side of the road. One had a green roof and a windmill out in front and a white picket fence. Suddenly a car loomed in sight. An old Packard sedan. I practically flagged it down.

"Going to Frisco, mister?"

"Sure."

The guy behind the wheel was a hawk-faced, peppy old gent with a radio going and a cigarette dangling from the side of his mouth. "I'll take you in," he said.

I sat in the middle, next to him, Emmie on the outside. The old guy almost stripped the gears starting off.

"Nice day," he said.

"Yeah."

He burped and pardoned himself and patted his stomach. "You live in Frisco?"

I shook my head. "We got a farm back there." I said this because if he'd heard about two people wanted by cops he wouldn't connect it with Emmie and me. I wanted him to think we were farmers. "My name's Joe Franklin," I said. "This is my wife, Hilda."

"Glad to meet 'cha," he said. Then: "What kind of crops you growing this year?"

I thought quick. "Tomatoes mostly. We got quite a few string beans, and cabbages—and of course the orange trees."

He nodded thoughtfully. "You getting good prices?"

"Well, average, I guess." I turned to Emmie. "Wouldn't you say the prices were average, Blondie?"

"Well—a—" Emmie said and gulped. Her whole face reddened.

"You call your wife 'Blondie'?" the dope asked chuckling, and I knew I was doing a good job throwing him off.

"Yeah. It's a pet name I have for her. She's a natural blonde. She doesn't use any of that peroxide stuff."

He leaned over the wheel and looked at Emmie. She still had on that scarf, and you couldn't tell whether her hair was black or white.

"I like light hair," he said.

"Then the kids," I went on. "They take after their mother. They're little toe-heads. Annie she's four now—her hair's like ripe wheat."

"It's nice to have kids," the guy said. "I got one myself."

"Hell," I said, "I got four. Little devils. Phil and Roger—they're regular devils. The other day they almost drowned one of my pigs."

"You got pigs, too?"

"Sure. One cow, twelve pigs. I got a whole slew of chickens too."

"You got some farm."

"Yeah," I sighed, "me and the little woman—we work awful hard."

"What you going to do in Frisco?" he asked abruptly.

"Well, you see, we—we couldn't take the Cadillac because I used up all the gas coupons. Hell, I only got an A book. But in Frisco, we're going to, first, the doctor's office. You see I hurt my foot plowing. One of the horses stepped on my instep."

He turned and looked at me. "You got horses, too?"

"Sure. Five of 'em. I got a hell of a lot of mouths to feed."

"You sure have."

"Then from the doctor's office, we're going to take a bus and cruise around a while and come home. Maybe take in a picture show."

"Sort of a day out, eh?"

"Well, sort of. We haven't been away from the farm for five months, have we, Hilda?" When I turned to Emmie she was staring at me. "Have we, Blondie?" I repeated and nudged her.

She didn't come in quick enough, so I went on: "Yeah—at least five months—maybe six."

I kept up this line of gab. He asked me all kinds of questions about farming. I didn't know what he was talking about half the time, but I faked my way through.

Pretty soon we passed Palo Alto, then we were on the ridge road, water on both sides. We entered the city. First Wop Town, then you could see the Twin Peaks.

Every road seemed to lead to Market Street—with its four lines of car tracks. It ran along at the bottom of a steep hill and there were cable cars at the footing, getting ready to take passengers back up the vertical climb. I noticed the buildings were compact, set tight against each other.

The Packard turned on one of the main streets. The guy stopped, and Emmie and I got out. I said:

"Thanks, mister. Any time you're driving through again—you stop in at the farm and see Hilda and me—"

"What's the address?"

"Well—" I said, "it's the first farmhouse past the crossroads—right there where you picked us up. The one with the green roof and a windmill out in front."

He said: "Has it got a white picket fence around the lawn?"

"Yeah—that's the one."

"I sure will stop." His voice got excited. "I been stopping there every day for ten years. I live there!"

My tongue felt loose in my mouth. "Oh, it isn't on the *main* highway," I blurted. "It's about two miles down."

He was eying me suspiciously. "I don't know what your game is—but you're no farmer. And don't let me ever catch you around my place, you lying son of a—"

I made a flying leap for the running board, but he'd already gassed the heap, and he was off. I went back to Emmie. "Can you imagine the nerve of that guy!"

I saw that she was trembling. She stood there on the sidewalk, staring up at me. It was just beginning to get dark and people were hurrying past us.

"Never," she said limply, "never in my whole life, have I heard anyone make up things so easily. How *could* you tell those lies so fast, so—*effortlessly!* I—I can't believe it. I can't believe my ears! Actually I—"

"Well for Christ's sake—don't make a production out of it! Do you want the cops trailing us, do you? I was only covering tracks, trying to be smart about it."

"You were smart, all right. You just made the man more suspicious. If you'd kept still...."

"Can't a guy make a mistake!"

"Please, darling—don't raise your voice like that!"

"Forget it, Emmie Let's go get some chow."

18

We had dinner in a side street beanery—then we started out to find a room for the night. We went from hotel to hotel. Emmie stayed outside while I approached the desk clerks. It was the same story everywhere: filled to capacity. Servicemen were curled up on couches and easy chairs in some of the lobbies, sound asleep.

We walked on.

I thought we'd left the fog back in Walton. I was wrong. It was so thick in Frisco that night it rolled through the streets in gray formless puffs. Traffic hummed through it, headlights dimmed.

I pulled my collar up around my neck. It was October, but men were wearing overcoats. The cold reminded me of the blizzard weather back in Ohio. It wasn't snowing here of course, but it was the same kind of cold: raw and penetrating.

We passed the Army and Navy Y.M.C.A.—soldiers lolling all over the stone steps in front. We went down to the Embarcadero—a long, wide street near the waterfront. From here you could see the Golden Gate Bridge silhouetted against the skyline, cars crawling across. There were ships in the harbor, sea gulls with outstretched wings, voices squawking.

All at once I saw the uniform: a cop, coming toward us. He was tall and wide with a scar across his cheek. I grabbed Emmie's arm—and we pretended to be looking in a store window. There were all kinds of Chinese herbs piled up on display, with cards telling the different kinds. But I wasn't studying the names; I was watching this cop's every move through the corner of my eye.

He stopped in back of us and rubbed his face and looked back. He saw us and came over to the window. He started to peer in between us at the display. I was ready to make a lunge when he turned abruptly and sauntered on. Then Emmie and I were on our way.

We passed bars, stumble bums, merchant sailors of all nationalities. Navy sailors, tough-looking women—white-faced, red-lipped. Russians, Chinese, Filipinos. You could hear the hoarse muddle of sound from the ferryboat horns, the blaring noise of the juke boxes. People, crowds, bums ... a Salvation Army guy ringing his tambourine.

We passed a dark stairway. *Beds—25 cents. No vacancy.* At the corner I bought a newspaper and looked up the street. There was a third-rate hotel about a block up. It looked pretty good from the outside. We hurried up to it.

The desk clerk said he had two rooms left, so I signed a phony John-Henry. I had to put down a previous address so I gave Tulsa, Oklahoma. It was the first place that came to my mind. It cost me three bucks for two, for the night—but I guess it'd been more if it hadn't been for the ceiling price. The clerk handed me a key marked 206.

The room was small and damp, with a ratty blue carpet and scuffed furniture. Fog-soaked curtains hung at the window. There was a small private shower room to one side, no bathtub. A brawl was going on in the room next to us. You could hear the loud talking and swearing. Some dame on a drunken crying jag. She kept blubbering and the guy kept telling her to pipe down.

Emmie pulled the scarf off her head and sank down on the bed. I noticed her suit was pretty badly wrinkled, and she looked tired—with a trace of dark circles under her eyes. She kicked off her shoes and rested her head back.

I jerked off my tie. Then I saw the gas heater, and lighted it. Emmie got up and stood before the fire rubbing her hands. I got the newspaper out of my pocket and scanned every page, each item. There was no mention of Stella Flint or the town of Walton. I counted out the money in my pocket. I had four dollars and sixty-three cents left. I said:

"We got to go to the bank first thing in the morning and draw out that dough—" I said it in an offhand manner, but I knew as soon as I laid hands on the mazuma I'd drop her quick. I'd go on up to Reno maybe, try my luck at the tables.

Emmie moved back to the bed and sat down again. She was silent for a moment, then she said, "Isn't it dangerous to try and get that money?"

"Sure it is. But it's a chance we have to take. We got to have dough."

She sat up and unfastened her stockings from her garter belt and pulled them off. I noticed her legs. White and smooth—not too muscular, I thought, but kind of nice.

"But the bank employees here will check with the Walton bank," she said slowly.

"Sure. So what? They'll only verify that you've got that much dough. You'll be out of the bank with the ten grand before Judd can find out."

She didn't like the idea. She said, "Can't you get some of your money somehow?"

"You know I can't, Emmie. Wiring my broker means giving a return address. Now wouldn't that be a sweet way for the cops to pick us up!"

Her voice went weak. "You want me to go in the bank—alone?"

"It's your dough, isn't it?"

"But darling, I can't draw it out tomorrow."

I was losing patience fast. "No? Why not?"

"Tomorrow is Sunday. The bank's closed."

I stared at her. I swore under my breath. It meant I'd have to stick around one more day.

Emmie stepped out of her skirt. She took off her jacket and blouse, then took them over to the closet and hung them up. She walked over to the dresser in her slip, got a comb out of her purse and ran it through her hair. After that she broke out a toothbrush and stood over the wash basin washing her teeth.

I thought: leave it to a woman to jab a toothbrush in her pocket—even when she's running away from cops!

I noticed her slenderness, then I saw the contours: snug waist, lovely breasts. She distracted my thoughts. I sat fascinated, watching her. Nice body, full and athletic—wide shoulders, slim hips. Nice hair, too. Rich, brown, shiny. She was pinning it on top of her head. She wrapped a bath towel around it and fastened the towel together with a hairpin.

"My shower cap," she said.

She stepped into the small shower room and closed the curtain tight. One hand threw out her slip and underclothes. I heard the water going full blast.

I stared at the closed curtain. I asked myself what I was doing here. The dough, of course. For a second I'd forgotten the dough....

The running water stopped abruptly. I heard her drying herself, saw the curtain bulge.

"Darling—will you give me my slip?"

I was all hands picking it up.

She came out then, with the slip back on, carrying the towel, her hair all loose again. "I'll have to sleep in my slip," she said shyly. She went over to the bed, pulled back the covers and got in.

I watched her face. She looked tired but her eyes were glowing. I noticed her teeth were white and even. It was as though I'd never seen her before.

"B-rr. What cold sheets. Darling—come to bed."

Who, me? I almost said. "In a second, Emmie. I got to take a shower, too."

I was out of the shower in three minutes flat. I turned off the light, but the gas made red and purple reflections across the wall. Outside the window fog drifted by, thick and murky. The arguing from behind the thin partition was still coming over. A radio was playing in there, and the dame was singing in a husky contralto. The guy kept telling her she had a lousy voice. He was right.

A news broadcast came over. I glued my ear to the wall, careful not to miss any word. It went on about the war, and then there was dance music. It clicked off abruptly. The door in the next room opened and closed. The couple had gone out. All at once you could hear the ferryboat whistles, the seagulls—now and then voices from the street below.

"It's nice and warm in here now," Emmie said.

"Yeah." I got in bed beside her.

She put her arms around me and I felt a sudden twinge of self-consciousness. Then my lips were on hers. My blood felt warm. We held on to each other, and she said:

"I'm not afraid—anymore. We have each other, darling, and that's all that can ever matter."

I pulled her closer.

She said: "It isn't wrong for us to run away—is it?"

I kissed her again, and she began to cry.

I saw her face in the reflection of the gas light. She was my wife. I'd never had a wife before, but it seemed good: as good as sunlight and starlight and music and whatever else you can think of that's good in this world.

"Emmie—" I said, and then I couldn't say any more. I was just holding her there in my arms, and I thought: it's a crazy world. It sure as hell is a crazy world!

19

I remember later that night—Emmie shaking me, whispering hoarsely in my ear:

"Eric—somebody's at the door—"

I bolted up and threw back the covers. I heard the knocking. It was at our door all right. Loud and insistent....

Judd!

He'd caught up with me! I could see him standing outside. *Calm, cool, collected.* He'd say: "*It didn't take me long, Stanton!*"

I ran to the window, looked out. It was a fifteen-foot jump to the street. I'd try it. I'd try anything to keep out of his clutches! I groped my way back to the closet and began throwing on my clothes.

The knock sounded again, louder.

The guy next door was back in his room. He yelled: "Pipe down out there! People got to sleep!"

I heard voices in the hall. *How many cops did he bring with him!*

I was conscious of Emmie beside me, fumbling for her clothes. She'd taken her cue from me.

"Mister Spruce?" a masculine voice said from outside. That was the phony name I'd given. It didn't fool me for a minute. It was Judd's voice. He'd been checking all the hotels in town: "*Did a girl and a man register here tonight? He's about six foot, dark complected, dark brown eyes. The girl's—*"

"Mister Spruce?" the voice said again, impatient this time.

"Just a minute," I said. I was stalling, getting on my shirt. I didn't stop to button it. I grabbed up my coat.

"I'd like to see you a minute—"

"Be right there," I managed.

Emmie had on her suit and shoes. She had her underclothes and stockings in her hand.

"Through the window," I whispered.

She ran over to it and gasped at the jump ahead. But she was ready to go. She had one foot on the sill waiting for me to say when.

"It's the manager, Mister Spruce," the voice outside went on. "I'm sorry to bother you, but the marine's here who occupied the room last night. He has to ship out right away and he just remembered he left some money under the throw rug. If you'll be kind enough to—"

Pretty clever, Judd! I kicked the rug over on my way to the window. I felt under the carpet and I felt the greenbacks. I held them up to the splotchy moonlight. It was dough all right. Twenty-dollar bills. Three of them.

I thought: Judd couldn't have *planted* the dough there! It *was* the manager!

I slipped off my coat and hurried over to the door. Some guy whispered:

"I only got ten minutes to get on board."

I turned the key and opened the door.

The manager was a little blonde guy with a moustache. He came inside and brushed past me before I could hand him the dough. The marine was a young kid with bloodshot eyes. He saw the dough in my hand and grabbed it. He counted it fast.

"It's all here," he said and heaved a sigh. "Gee, thank you, sir."

"Sorry to disturb you," the manager said, and then the two of them had gone.

I turned around to Emmie. *She wasn't there!* I ran to the window, peered down, expecting to see her lying in a heap on the pavement. It was a hell of a drop; she was unconscious maybe! I could feel the slow heavy beat of my heart.

I heard footsteps behind me. It was Emmie—stepping out of the shower room.

"Eric, you're pale as a sheet!"

I felt choked up. For a moment I couldn't speak. "I'm okay," I said finally.

But even after we undressed and got back in bed I still had the shakes.

The radio from the next room was going full blast when I woke up—a Sunday morning church program. I opened my eyes and saw Emmie—on her knees by the side of the bed, her eyes looking heavenward.

"Amen," she said softly.

I said, "Did you send one up for me?"

She got up and bent over and kissed my forehead. "Several, darling. I prayed that Mister Judd wouldn't find you. That was one, and—"

"I hope that one works."

She smiled down at me, "And Clara—I prayed she—" She broke off, tears welling in her eyes.

"Clara's okay. Stop worrying." I got out of bed.

"Why can't the police find out who killed Stella Flint?" She paused. "I've been thinking, Eric, if Atkins didn't kill her, could it have been the restaurant man?"

"Pop? I doubt it."

"Then who could have done it?"

I shrugged.

"It's awfully strange—I mean, *somebody* killed her."

"Yeah."

We talked about stuff like that, then later we had breakfast in the hotel café, but not together. Emmie left first and when she came up I went downstairs and ate. I didn't think it was such a good plan for us to be seen together. Cops would be looking for a couple.

In the afternoon we read the newspaper and listened to the radio news reports through the partition, and the dame who'd been on the crying jag last night was moaning about how sick she was and asking the guy to go find some ice to make the water colder. She kept it up all day long. By evening, I'd smoked so many cigarettes my mouth was raw inside. I felt if I had to stay cooped up in the room for a minute longer I'd go nuts.

"Let's go have chow and see a show," I told Emmie. "We can buy our tickets separately."

She started looking through the theatrical page of the newspaper.

"Never mind that," I said. "We can't be particular. There's a theatre around the corner. We'll take pot luck."

Her eyes came up. "Look, darling—Ernest Madley is here in San Francisco."

"Madley?"

She nodded. "The spiritual medium—you know, the one who came to Walton. He gave me a message from—"

"Oh, yeah. Sure," I said.

"It says 'Last Week—Ebell Clubhouse.'"

"I guess he doesn't always make one-night stands."

She looked up at me, her eyes bright. "Eric—I've just thought of a marvelous idea—"

"Yeah?"

"*You're* a medium—you communicate with the dead. Why can't you talk to Stella Flint—*ask* her who *killed* her?"

I stared at her. Was she crazy? But I saw she actually expected an answer. "Hell," I said, "I've thought of that. It's—it's—"

"It's what, darling?"

I thought fast. "Well, it's this way. You see, when a person dies, he—well, he travels through a planetary sphere, as it were, that is to say, it's impossible for them to come through—until they're at least a year old."

She studied me curiously. "But Ernest Madley talks to them. I remember at the séance—Josephine Potter died only two months ago—and Madley talked to *her*—"

"Well, yes—" I was sweating. "But you see—I was referring to people who die from unnatural causes. There's a difference. Take people who've been murdered and the like, take them— It isn't natural to be murdered, is it?"

"No."

"Of course not, and getting them to come through is a difficult thing, you see?"

"I don't believe I do, dear."

I talked faster. "Well, people who are murdered, people who commit suicide, criminals who are electrocuted—they're all in one class. They're sensitive, backward. Their astral bodies sort of hover over—" I blew up suddenly. "Christ, Emmie—I'm telling you they won't come through!"

"You don't have to shout at me, dear. I'm only trying to understand."

"Then use your head. Anybody knows that a spirit who was murdered in earthly life can't come through and tell who killed him. What would be the use of courts or lawyers or judges or juries—if that was all that needed to happen—a spirit telling who murdered him. Don't you see, there's a law of balance that governs everything."

She nodded thoughtfully. "I guess it's all too deep for me."

And me, I thought. "Come on, Emmie, let's get the hell out of here—let's go to the show!"

I had the itches.

20

On Monday morning we walked back to Market Street, Emmie several feet behind me. Then we had breakfast in a coffee shop, sitting up at the counter, and I could see through the plate glass window outside. I could see the big sign all across the building across the street. It said:

Bank of America.

I watched people going in and out while I lapped up every crumb of my bacon and eggs. But Emmie sort of picked at her food. She looked tired again this morning, like she hadn't slept any too good.

"Eat up," I told her.

She smiled nervously. "The food just won't go down."

"Emmie, you're not *robbing* the bank," I said exasperated. "That's *your* dough!"

"I know, darling. I'm being ridiculous. But what if they hold me there after they check with the Walton bank, what if they—"

"Don't start that all over again!" I'd heard nothing else all morning.

"Well, I—" She saw my expression. "I guess I'm just jittery, that's all. I'll go now, dear." She got up. "I feel better already." Her face was pale, her eyes scared.

I watched her go out the door. Then she was lost with the pedestrians crossing the street. I glimpsed her going in the bank entrance. I looked up at the café clock. Ten-thirty....

It was going to be easy, I told myself. First I'd get her to hand me the dough for safekeeping. Second, we'd go back to the hotel room. I'd go out on some pretext or other. Then I'd come running back and tell her I just saw Judd on the street. I had to scram, fast! Alone. I'd tell her to go back to Walton and wait till I got in touch with her. Third, I'd be so excited I'd naturally forget to give her any of her money.

I thought about that and watched the bank entrance. Suddenly my thoughts were interrupted. A police car was pulling up in the red zone in front. I got an uneasy feeling, but then, I reasoned, cops had bank accounts as well as anyone else. My mind went back to Emmie, to how easy it was going to be now to get the dough.

It was one, two, three. I'd play it out like an actor. It was one clean sweep. Emmie'd have no hard feelings. She'd go back to Walton and wait. Maybe, like Clara, she'd wait forever, but she could have no hard feelings. She'd know I skipped with her dough all right, but under the circumstances she'd never know whether or not it was intentional.

Painless extraction ... nobody got hurt. I was glad now that things turned out the way they had. The smoothest part of it was that Emmie'd never know she was the sucker. That was the part I liked.

I noticed the clock again. Five minutes to eleven.... She'd been gone twenty-five minutes. I got squeamish, ordered another cup of coffee, smoked another cigarette.

Then it happened. The cops were back outside, only they weren't alone. *Emmie was between them!* One cop had hold of her arm. She was crying! A group was gathering on the sidewalk, watching the cops help her into the back seat of the police car!

I sat there petrified for a split second, conscious of my heart chugging unevenly. Panic swept through me. I didn't wait. I was on my feet, making for the kitchen.

A waitress was giving the cook an order. A dishwasher grinned up at me toothlessly. I shot past them out the door. A moment later I was running down the alley, my brain full of sirens.

No panic, I told myself. *Take it easy, pal. Take it awfully easy!*

I saw a streetcar at the corner. I hurried over to it and got lost with the people boarding the platform. I fished around in my pocket and found a dime. My hands were shaking like palsy. My legs carried me to the front. I sat down in back of the conductor and the street car moved slowly on, bells clanging.

I was shaking all over.

Judd's work ... he'd spread a net all right. He was out to get me! Instead he got Emmie!

Then I thought of something that made me sick to my stomach. The dough—gone, vanished! All the time I'd built up to it, and now it was gone! I wasn't scared anymore. I was hot, shaking with rage.

I reached down in my pocket and brought up the loose change. I counted it, and then I stared at the coins in my palm.
Eighty-seven cents left! Eighty-seven goddam, lousy cents!
I got sicker.
I don't know how long I rode that streetcar. I don't know how I managed to sit there. I remember it was crowded: kids, dames, workmen, stink. I rode to the end of the line, then I began to walk unaware of direction.

I thought about the cops who picked Emmie up. She'd probably tell them the name of the hotel where we'd stayed. She hadn't as much as glanced across the street to the coffee shop. She hadn't given me away. She knew I saw the cops pick her up.

So right about now cops were looking for me at the hotel. They were searching the waterfront, the dives. The best thing I could do was find myself a place to hide.

But what was I going to use for dough!

I saw a rack of newspapers at the corner. I picked up one and combed the pages. There was still no mention of the murder. Why was everything so quiet!

I walked on, down to Golden Gate Park. I didn't know what to do with myself. I sat down on a bench, with a dull hollowness inside me, and watched people: a sailor and a dame. The two of them were holding hands and she had a dreamy stare in her eyes.

She sort of reminded me of Emmie. Not her looks—her eyes. It was the way Emmie looked at me: bright headlights—all love and adoration. I laughed a little bit thinking about that—the way she thought I was a good guy. And suddenly I wasn't laughing. When Judd filled her ears, she'd know me all right. She'd know everything I ever told her was a lie. The sucker would be enlightened.

I shrugged it off and got up again.

At the corner I went into a drugstore, sat up at the counter and ate a sandwich and malt. The check came to forty-five cents. It said to pay the cashier. I got up and went over to the tobacco counter.

A little bald-headed guy stood behind the cash register. I ordered a pack of Luckies. He just looked at me like I was crazy. "What are Luckies?" he said. He was a cute baby, this one. I asked him if he had any hair tonic called Wheelers—or Whiting—or something like that. I told him it began with a W. He scratched his head in thought and I gave him the old routine:

"My wife's right out front in the car," I said. "Just a minute—I'll ask her the name of it."

Another customer came up to pay his check and I beat it outside. I hadn't paid the guy a cent. I kept walking.

When it got dark I took a streetcar back to the city. I got off at the Fox theatre and walked from there all the way down to the ferry building. I sauntered past the cigar and candy booths with their toys and souvenirs. There were newspaper kids shouting headlines, crowds of soldiers and sailors, some of them going back to the Navy Yard at Vallejo—others coming in on leave. A lot of servicemen were asleep on the benches. I found a seat and sat down, feeling awkward and out of place with all those uniforms.

I watched the sliding ads as they turned over, making a monotonous click. Little neon signs advertising tobacco, soap and razor blades. People kept milling past, whole families going to work in the mills, carrying kids, kids asleep in their arms.

Ferries going everywhere ... Sacramento, Treasure Island, Oakland, Vallejo. A peanut vendor moved listlessly through the crowd, mumbling to himself.

I watched the S.P.'s in their leggings, white belts, billies in hand, asking to see liberty cards. Over by the door an M.P. stood in his khaki uniform, leggings, his eyes surveying everybody who passed in and out.

I saw the soldier framed in the doorway. He piped the M.P. and turned his face away quick. He started to beat it back outside, but it was too late. The M.P. had spotted him and was hurrying out the door.

I got up and moved to where I could see what was happening. The soldier was fumbling in his pocket for his identification. His right arm suddenly came up, but the M.P. had been ready. He stepped back, then he had the soldier's arms pinned behind him. Two more M.P.'s came on the run. One of them reached in the soldier's pocket and brought out his identification. They looked at it and hauled the guy off.

I sat back down on the closest bench, feeling dizzy. It was the look on the soldier's face that got me. Stark white in panic. A deserter, probably. The cops had caught up with him....

Suddenly I felt cold. I went outside, then I was walking. Fog everywhere, wet and gray. Something was gnawing inside me—like hunger. I passed a hot dog stand and bought a sandwich for a dime. But I could only gulp down half of it. The other half I wrapped in the paper napkin and stuck in my pocket. It would be my breakfast. Seventy cents remaining....

I tried laughing it off. So what? I told myself. You've been broke all your life. What the hell, you act like it's some kind of novelty. You can always scrape up dough!

Seventy cents! Why didn't I buy myself an apartment house....

My mind worked like that. My mind was haywire. I couldn't think, or reason things out. I knew something was wrong. The old ego was missing. I wasn't bitter anymore about losing the dough. I felt soft, spongy. *I felt so goddam alone!* At least with Emmie I had somebody to talk to. I had a good roof over my head.

I had a roof now. The foggy, black sky of all San Francisco. I had seventy cents. I had a lot of company waiting: cops.

If I don't talk to somebody soon I'll go nuts!

Why don't you go nuts? My mind said. They'll put you away in a quiet asylum. They'll bring you food on a tray. They'll lock you in a room away from all cops....

I found myself on Third Avenue, the bowery of San Francisco. There was an all-night theatre. I bought a ticket, fifteen cents, and went inside, sat down next to a seedy-looking bum. He was sprawled all over the seat, his head resting back, his mouth agape in sleep. It was warm in there at least, better than a park bench.

There was loud snoring behind me. Some other guy sleeping. *Grand Hotel.* People come, people go.

The noise from the screen ground on. It was an old film, scratchy in places. Probably made when talkies first came in. I opened my peepers and caught a flash of the scene. It was a gangster's hide-out. Five tough-looking hombres draped throughout the room, discussing the best way to get rid of the body.

I closed my eyes again. These Hollywood writers, I thought, you got to hand it to them. Gangsters never thought of putting their victim's legs in cement and tossing them in the river until they first saw it on the screen.

I wondered how Emmie was doing. Probably on her way to Walton by now—escorted by the police. They'd hold her as an accomplice. That was pretty bad. She was on a spot, that's what she was. She wasn't like those hard-boiled dames who could look out for themselves.

Here she was—living with a crazy sister and looking for her prince. And finally she finds him. At last she thinks she's found a home and a husband—then she finds out.... It was kind of like a story, she—

Christ! I thought, why don't you stop! What are you worrying about it for? What does it mean to you? Since when do you consider the sucker's viewpoint!

Still she was kind of a nice little dame when you came down to it. I mean—strictly for a guy who was content to sit by the fire with his pipe and magazines. It sounded good in stories—the little wife baking the biscuits and all. Ordinary people.

I thought about the way she looked after me, did little things for me—the way she thought I was a good guy. Things she said, I remembered: *"I couldn't believe even a little thing bad about you!"* The way she held on to me: *"Take me with you, Eric. Please, please! I must go with you!"* And last night she'd said: *"We have each other, darling, and that's all that can ever matter."*

How did you figure a dame like that? Christ, why was I feeling so all alone! I didn't give a damn about her, but what was wrong with me? Why was I in such high gear—so nervous it was an effort to sit still!

I knew I felt something. I couldn't describe it—or understand it. I didn't know what it was. All I could do was fight against it. It was a setup for the suckers, and that didn't include me.

I smelled the reek of the theatre, the putrid, close air. *What was I doing here!* I should be making my way out of Frisco. I should be on a passenger bus headed for—anywhere.

But cops were anywhere too, and everywhere. No matter where I went I'd be dodging around corners, holding my breath in fear of a tap on the shoulder. All because of Judd, his hunch that I killed—

"But you can't keep running away—"

The words jerked me straight up in my seat. They'd come from the screen. A brunette dame was pleading with a guy. He was a shady-looking character; evidently he was hiding out in her room. His eyes kept glancing to the door.

"I took the chance of coming up here," he said. "I had to say good-bye." His face was all agony.

She was crying suddenly. "But you can't always keep running away," she said and she was a pretty good little actress. "Nothing is so bad if you stop and face it. Cowards run and run, but sane men go back! You have to stop and face it! You can't keep on running away!"

The words seared through me. *You can't keep running away ... you have to face things sometime....*

"Stop torturing yourself," she went on. "You only die once. And you—you're dying a thousand deaths each day."

"You're talking crazy," he told her. "The cops think I was in on the bank robbery. I wasn't. If you think I'm going to take the rap for—"

She threw her arms around him and pleaded some more. But it was no soap. The guy beat it out, down the fire escape. Then it showed a montage of his slow degradation, how he sunk from bad to worse. He wound up picking up cigarette butts from the street, bumming dimes. His face aged twenty years. Finally in a snow blizzard the guy ended up keeling over dead in the gutter. It was the end of the picture.

I sat there for a long time thinking about it. The dame was right. He should have faced it, maybe tried to prove somehow that he wasn't in on the bank robbery.

But I guess it's that way with some people. I knew all my life I'd been a coward. I'd been afraid to face things.

I remembered the night I'd told Stella how I ran away from home when I was thirteen—because my old man put the heat on me. That was true—but I didn't tell her the reason he worked me over so much. It was because I was always getting in trouble and beating it off somewhere.

Jesus! The day I stole the dollar out of my mother's purse. I was afraid to go home. I knew she'd missed the buck.

It was snowing that night. I walked three miles through it, up to town. I tried not to think how cold it was or how afraid I was to go home. My feet began to sting. It was effort to lift them, but I finally got to the theatre, and that was where my old man caught me. He beat me all the way home.

After I was in bed, I bawled for a while, then I started thinking. The welts on me weren't half as bad as that walking around in the snow shivering.

I thought: I should have gone home in the first place, instead of being so afraid. If I had, I wouldn't be hungry now, and my feet wouldn't be hurting. And the next day I wouldn't have had pneumonia again—like I did.

But I still couldn't see it.

Later, I stole a fountain pen and got caught. The teacher gave me a note to take home, and that was the last I ever saw of her, or my parents either. I hopped the rails that afternoon. Two months later I was in Mexico.

I remember the old Mexican guy who took me in—when I caught pneumonia again. He took care of me. I got to know where he stashed his dough. One night I borrowed the roll—about sixty bucks. I went to the gambling house and lost the whole shebang at the crap table.

I left Mexico that night.

That night was twelve years ago, but it might as well have been six or four or one or one month or one week. It was always the same. I guess all my life I'd gotten into jams and ran away. It was the same in L.A. I'd beat it out before the sheriff got me. I was always one step ahead of myself. Trouble came in and I went out.

My whole life might have been different if I'd faced things. I was sick of running, always running away from something.

Now at twenty-eight, it was no different.

I was still on the run.

21

I left the theatre feeling hot inside, feverish. My head hurt, my lungs ached, my eyes felt sunken in their sockets. There was nothing but misery all through me. I didn't know where I was, coming or going or in the fog or in the rain or sitting in the sun or walking in the street or in the moonlight or what. I saw the stores, people: I must've been walking. Something inside me was yelling. It kept yelling:

Why'd you run away from Judd!

I knew why. I was afraid. But I was away from him now—and I was still afraid. It didn't make sense. What if he did send me up! *You only die once!* I'd been dying ever since I was eight! I'd be great in a war. The first time I heard a gun go off I'd run. *I'm tired of running*, I told myself. *I don't want to run anymore!* The thought nagged, kept nagging. *I didn't kill Stella! I didn't! I didn't!*

"I'm innocent," I said aloud.

A little runt bum was walking beside me. He gave my shoulder a pat.

"Sure, you're innocent," he said.

"But I am," I said. "I *am!* You can't run away forever!" I felt a burning in my stomach.

The little bum patted my shoulder again. "Don't I know it," he said and hurried on.

I stared after him. I walked into a restaurant. My stomach felt like acid, and the gnawing was still there. I sank back in the counter chair. A waiter stood before me, expecting an order.

"Ham and eggs," I blurted.

I turned to the vacant chair next to me: *What'll you have, Emmie?*

She wasn't there.

Little things about her kept coming back to me—the way she looked when I first saw her at the organ. That night in the trailer camp, in her yellow satin nightgown, her hair tied back. The way she always tried to do little things for me ... and now

Judd had her!

Judd, Judd, Judd! He was trying to pin the murder rap on me. I was as smart as he. Why couldn't *I* pin it on somebody else—uncover things—find evidence enough to send somebody up!

There's a way out! You've got to think!

Why was Stella killed? What was the motive? A motive could be most anything. Jealousy, greed, hate, fear. I had to have a scent—and follow it.

Atkins ... maybe he *was* guilty! He'd said he bought gas at a service station in Fulton at two in the morning. The attendant remembered him, verified his story. But what kept the attendant from accepting a bribe to say that. A hundred bucks or two or five hundred. Five hundred bucks would tempt a guy to remember anything.

Atkins wasn't picked up till late the following night. What kept him from contacting the service station guy and fixing up the alibi! Did Judd ever think of that? And why didn't Stella tell me she knew Atkins—in Arizona? Was she afraid of what I might do? Or was there something else she didn't want me to know....

I considered Pop. Why had he been so concerned about Stella? When she came back to work for him, he fell all over himself—he was that glad to see her. He bought her perfume—expensive perfume—*why?* He said he didn't buy her the jewelry. If he did buy it, why'd he lie about it? Maybe he was dumb like a fox. Judd found out Pop bought the perfume through sales slips he found in Stella's room. Where were the sales slips for the jewelry? It was bought out of town. Maybe that was what Pop did on those trips he made—buy her that jewelry! Then why did Stella tell me *she* bought that wristwatch she was wearing?

It was all questions, no answers. If I only had an answer!

Could Stella have meant Pop when she told me that somebody with dough wanted to marry her? Pop had dough. Plenty of it. Maybe it was Pop who was waiting for her in the shadows of the rooming house....

Why was he so *upset* about her death! Maybe Judd knew what he was talking about when he'd said Pop was in love with her, had eyes on her. You don't moon around for days like Pop did unless you're hit *hard!*

Yet, Pop was soft and softhearted. I remembered one day in the restaurant when he'd found a big spider in one of the cupboards. He'd coaxed it onto a paper and put it out the back door because he was too tender-hearted to kill it. He even shooed all the flies out of the joint instead of swatting them. To think he'd take a human life ... well, it was hard to swallow.

Why not Clara? You had to first think how a crazy mind works. Until I came along she'd had Emmie all to herself. I remembered something Emmie'd said once about the guys who tried to call on her.

"*Clara talks to them,*" she said, "*and they never come back.*"

Clara had a motive in keeping Emmie an old maid. If Emmie got married she'd be left alone, with no one to tell her ailments to. Nobody to sympathize with her, humor her. Since her husband left she'd made up her mind that men were no good. She'd made a point of keeping guys away from Emmie.

Clara didn't know about me at first, because Emmie met me outside. It wasn't until after she consented to marry me that she told her sister about me for the first time. Clara knew it was too late to squelch the marriage.

It was after Emmie moved out that Clara knew real loneliness. The house was empty and silent. Without Emmie, she became more and more afraid. Possessed with fear. Her demented mind thought of ways to get Emmie back.

Then the night she accidently passed the restaurant and saw me kissing Stella through the window—how did her mind work then? She could have decided to kill Stella! She would destroy her sister's menace. Maybe her own husband, Sam Reeder, had skipped off with another woman! She made up her mind that it wouldn't happen to Emmie!

A twisted mind has a strange way of reasoning. Maybe she thought I'd be blamed for the murder. Then Emmie would be rid of me; Emmie would then come home.

The landlady of the rooming house had told the police:

"*I heard Stella talking to somebody. I couldn't tell whether it was a man or a woman!*"

It was Clara who was waiting for her in the shadows of the rooming house! Stella couldn't take her to her room. No visitors were permitted after ten—she'd told me that once. The two of them went to the restaurant—maybe they argued for hours, and then—

Clara killed her! Clara picked up something and killed her!

I was trembling when the waiter set down the plate of ham and eggs. He wrote out a check. I pushed the plate away.

"I haven't the dough," I said.

He looked at me. "Go ahead and eat—you look like you need it."

I lapped up the food.

Proof ... evidence ... that was what I needed. I froze cold for a second: I knew exactly what I was going to do. I was going to clear myself of the blame for once and for all! Hell, I couldn't have a moment's peace with that rap hanging over my head!

I'm going back! I'm going back! I'm going back!

I kept saying it. I kept saying it and afterwhile I knew it was true. I was going back! But I knew I had to be clever about it. I had to be smart for the first time in my life.

Cops or no cops, I was going back to Walton!

22

It was getting daylight outside and the fog was lifting. I found the train yards and ducked the bulls. A farmer's freight was moving out. I grabbed it.

There were a lot of crates of vegetables and two guys in the boxcar. I asked where we were headed. L.A. one of the guys said. So I knew I was on the right track.

At San Luis Rey I got off and stalled for five hours. I didn't want to hit Walton till after dark. I ate lunch. It cost me forty-three cents. I left a twelve-cent tip on the counter, figuring I might as well be cleaned out flat. Then I hopped the rails again.

It was about nine-thirty when I jumped off near Walton. I cut across a field and kept on the outskirts of town. I cut down past the grocery store. The apartment upstairs looked strange and forlorn.

I walked on, past the little houses with their narrow yards, roofs shining in the darkness.

Two blocks up, I found the Barkley house. There was a light on in the front room. I hurried up the walk. On the porch, I stood motionless, listening. There was no sound from inside. I tapped on the door.

I waited for a full minute and tapped again. There was the sound of padded footsteps inside, then Clara's frightened voice:

"Y-yes?"

"It's the police, Mrs. Reeder—"

"The police?" Her voice came over shakily.

I heard the key turning in the lock. She opened the door just a crack.

"What do you want?" She said this before she peered out and saw me. Then she let out a moan.

I had one foot in the door.

"Eric—" she breathed. Her eyes looked like she was seeing a ghost.

She stepped back and I went inside, closing the door behind me. She stood frozen. She had on a bright pink robe and her hair was in that net again. She looked like she thought I was going to kill her.

I went over and flopped down in a chair. She relaxed a little. "Calm down," I told her. "Sit down and calm down."

Her eyes filled with childish terror. She backed up to the couch, not taking her gaze off me.

I wiped my hand down over my face, then looked up at her again. "Do you know the cops've got Emmie?"

"Do *I* know it?" She was sniveling. "Do *you* know the agony I've suffered until I knew tonight that the police had found her and brought her back?" She twisted a handkerchief in her hands, her face forlorn. "I've never been through such terrible suspense in my life! I was sure the police would find her mangled body in some horrible place! But she's safe—thank goodness—safe in jail!"

"She's in jail, eh?"

"Yes." She brought up one hand in a dramatic gesture. "Oh, but it's shameful. Her father would turn over in his grave if he knew. Emmie in jail!" She stared at me again. "What are you doing in this house? A *murderer* in this house!"

"Let's not be melodramatic, Clara. Just take it easy." I paused while she dabbed the handkerchief to her eyes. "You'd like to have Emmie back here, wouldn't you?"

She was hopeful. "Yes. Indeed I would. Is she—coming home tonight?"

"Maybe," I said. "It depends on you."

She was puzzled. "Me?"

I nodded. "You see, the police are only holding Emmie until they find out who killed Stella Flint."

Her thin face wrinkled. "They *know* who did it. It was *you!* The police are looking all over for you." Her eyes got scared again. "And here you sit in my front room!"

I got up and moved toward her.

"What—what are you going to do?" Her voice was faint, her whole body shaking.

"I didn't kill Stella," I said. "Understand?" I sat down on the couch beside her. "You see, I just had a little talk with one of the cops, and do you know what he told me?"

"No." She shrunk away from me.

"*He said he saw you in the restaurant the night of the murder!*" I dragged the words out, slow and deliberate.

Her eyes got glassy. "He *did?*"

I felt a burning excitement. "Yes, Clara. He also said he saw you waiting for Stella when she came home that night."

Her voice lowered to a whisper. "He said that? He said he saw me?"

I nodded. Every muscle inside me was tense. I was doing the staring now. Suddenly I was weak. I'd been right! It *was* Clara— her demented—

"Well, he's crazy!" she snapped. "I don't know what policeman told you that, but he's positively moonstruck!"

"You're trying to deny it?" I rasped.

She viewed me defiantly. "I was in bed that night. I didn't even know where that waitress lived. I can prove I was here—home at ten o'clock. You tell that policeman to ask Mrs. Harris." She pointed to the window. "She lives right there next door. I had a severe headache that night and I called Mrs. Harris over. She stayed with me all night." Her eyes flashed. "You just bring that policeman to see me!"

The wind had gone out of me. I got up and went back to the chair and sat facing her again. "Okay," I said weakly. "But I want to ask you one more question. Something that's always puzzled me."

She studied me curiously.

"Why didn't you tell Mister Judd you saw me kissing Stella on the night she was murdered?"

She thought a moment. "Why, I *promised* Emmie I wouldn't tell anybody." She paused. "Do you think I want my own sister *disgraced?*"

Reputation ... I thought. She wouldn't give cops any information that would blemish her sister's reputation.

"Okay," I said. I started for the door, then thought of something and turned back to her. "Clara, you've got to make me a promise. That you won't call the police after I've gone—"

"Well," she gulped.

"I'm trying to *help* Emmie. I'm trying to get her out of jail."

She nodded and bit her lip. She took a step toward me. "Then why don't you go to the police and confess?"

I was getting nowhere. "Look, Clara—I swear on a stack of—" I broke off. "You got a Bible here?"

"Indeed yes."

"Get it."

She hurried over to the mantel and came back holding it in her hands.

I said: "I swear by that Bible I didn't kill Stella."

She shook her head. "You didn't do it right."

"What'd you mean?"

"You must hold the Bible in your right hand while you're saying it, and afterwards kiss it—if you're telling the truth."

I took the book from her and held it in my right hand and repeated that I didn't kill Stella. Then I kissed the Bible. I said: "You've got to believe me. And if you go calling cops I'll never get Emmie out of jail." I paused for breath. "Do you promise you won't?"

She smiled at me. "Yes, I promise."

"Swear it on the Bible," I said.

She did.

"Thanks," I said drily.

I left the place feeling like I'd been through a wringer. I was nowhere. I was back where I started. If Clara *did* kill Stella she wasn't so batty after all. She was putting on a hell of a good act!

The air outside was icy cold. It stung my face and hands. I hurried down the street.

I've got to find out what happened to the Mexican, I thought, and Atkins. Pop would know. Pop was next on the agenda. I walked on, and I got to thinking. I was remembering words, scenes, fragments of scenes....

I thought of something that jarred me. *Why hadn't I thought of it before!* It was something Stella'd told me once—the night I first told her my plan of getting Emmie's dough. We were in the restaurant and I said something about hearing the kitchen stove simmering. Stella said she'd better go look *because once she was outside she couldn't get back in! She said she had no key!*

Then how did she get back in the restaurant the night of the murder—*unless Pop himself let her in!*

A trickle of sweat ran down my face. My eyes were burning, my throat felt parched and dry. *This was it!*
I hurried on down the street.

A light was on in the stucco house in front, blinds drawn. I walked on the lawn around to the side, to the smaller house in the rear. I stood for a moment in the shadows near the front porch, listening to the snoring from inside.

There was an open window leading off the porch. I studied it, figuring how I'd break in. I crept around to the back, looking for a piece of wire. There was an incinerator and a box of rubbish. I picked up a tin can lid. I hurried back to the front window and jabbed the tin through the screen. I worked my fingers through the slit and down to the hook and unloosened the screen. The snoring went on undisturbed.

I crawled through the window into the room, conscious of my own heavy breathing. I went through the small living room, through a doorway.

Moonlight shone on Pop's face, and over the bed where he lay. His mouth was open, and the snoring seemed to grow louder. The room was permeated with a reek of stale liquor. There was a bottle on the night stand beside his bed—half gone. I reached down and shook Pop gently.

He stirred, then he was snoring louder. I shook him again. He blinked up.

"Who is it? Who's here?"

"Quiet, Pop. Take it easy. You stay right where you are and be quiet and there won't be any trouble." My shadow was pale in the darkness.

His eyes flickered. "*You*, Eric? Is it you?"

"That's right."

He sat up quick. He was wide awake now. "Judd's lookin' for you. He's got everything turned inside out lookin' for you." He was talking a mile a minute. "They picked up your wife in Frisco. They got her in jail!"

"Yeah, I know."

He rubbed his eyes. "You seen today's paper?"

"No."

"They think *you* did it. They think *you* killed Stella." He paused, his eyes grew watery. "And you didn't, did you, Eric?"

"What do you think?"

"I know you didn't. You liked Stella too much."

"Yeah. What they doing with Emmie?"

He scratched his head. "I dunno. They think she knows where you are—and they're tryin' to find out." He shook his head. "It looks bad for you. Judd talks like he's sure you killed Stella."

"How about Atkins?" I said. "Did the cops let him go?"

Pop nodded. "But he's still in town. He says he's not leavin' till he finds out who killed Stella."

"And the Mexican? They still holding him?"

He thought a moment. "I dunno."

I said: "Look—I came here for a reason. I want the truth. Understand? I'm going to have to get pretty rough if I can't get the truth out of you—"

He looked up startled. "What'd you mean?"

I sat down on the edge of his bed and kept my eyes glued on him. "I've got proof," I said slowly, "it was *you* who let Stella back in the restaurant the night she was murdered."

He kept staring. "I—I don't know what you mean—"

"Then I'll repeat it, Pop. The night of the murder somebody saw you opening the restaurant door to let her in—"

He got excited. "I did not! I never went near there!"

"It *had* to be you. You see, she didn't have a key!"

His eyes were bulging; he kept panting for breath.

"She did too! I remember I gave her a key!"

"When?"

He thought again. "About a week before she was killed."

"*You're lying, Pop!* Stella worked for you for *six months!* Doesn't it strike you kind of funny that you'd give her a key *one week before she was killed!*"

He was trembling. "It's the truth!"

I held my voice low. "Why did you suddenly give her a key? She got along all right without one for six months!"

Tears trickled down his face. "Honestly, Eric—you don't think I harmed that girl. Do you?" His voice was anxious.

"You still haven't answered my question."

He looked at me strangely. "You've got me so flustered now I can't think straight." He rubbed his nose. "Lemme see, I gave her a key." He was babbling nervously. "I was plannin' on takin' a trip. You know I was. Well, I was thinkin' about it one day, so I gave her a key 'cause she'd have to look after things while I was gone." He paused. "When Mister Judd found the key in Stella's purse he gave it back to me."

My theory had evaporated into thin smoke. *If* Pop was telling the truth. But there was no way at all of my knowing.

"Pop," I said, "when you took those trips, you always brought her back some jewelry, didn't you? There's no use denying it because—"

"I never did!" He was indignant. "I always visited my brother, Sam. Sam lives in Glendale; he's older'n me, and he's—"

"Never mind." I was worn out suddenly, exhausted. "There's just one more thing—why didn't you tell me you knew what was going on between Stella and me—about how I was going to get some dough and take her away—"

"I don't know what you mean—"

"Judd found out about it. So she must've told you and you told Judd. That right?"

"I don't know what you mean," he repeated. "She never told me nothin' like that. If she was runnin' off again, I didn't know it."

"Listen, Pop—I want you to think very carefully. You've got to remember something. Did she ever tell you about a guy she knew that had dough? Somebody who wanted to marry her?"

"No. She never told me nothin'."

"Pop—you've got dough. I mean, quite a bit put away somewhere?"

He rubbed his hand over his mouth. "A little. Mebbe ten or fifteen thousand or so in the bank. Then I got some property and quite a few war bonds."

"Did you ever ask Stella to marry you?"

"You—you don't believe an old man like me—"

"*Answer me, Pop!*"

"You got more sense than to think that!"

"Then who was the guy she was talking about—the one who asked her to marry him?"

He shrugged.

"Pop, I want you to tell me who came in the restaurant to see her—besides Atkins and myself—"

He looked at the wall. Finally he said: "Nobody else. That bus driver used to come in all the time, but I ain't seen him since Stella came back to work."

"Did the cops ever pick him up for questioning?"

"I don't think so."

"Who else came in the restaurant?"

"Well —" He scratched his head. "Then that spiritualist fella'— you know, the one—"

"Madley?" I said.

He nodded. "That's his name. I ain't seen him lately but he used to come in regular and talk to Stella."

My voice grew excited. "You mean—even *after* the meeting—he stayed in town and came in after that?"

"Yep."

"You're *sure* of that, Pop?"

"Yep."

My throat was so tight I couldn't swallow.

"I don't know who it was that asked her to marry him," Pop went on. "'Course you got to remember Stella talked big. Maybe it was nobody, just somethin' she made up." He paused. "Maybe it was the one who kept writin' her letters—"

"Letters?" My pulse quickened. "Who wrote her letters?"

"I dunno. I just kept 'em and never read 'em."

"You kept them?"

He nodded. "I figure they're personal, and I didn't even let the cops see 'em. It's none of their business."

"Pop," I breathed, "you still got those letters?"

"You bet. I kept 'em away from cops and everybody. Judd asked me if I knew of any other personal effects she had and I told him no—because letters are private."

"I've got to see those letters!"

He folded his arms across his chest. "Nobody can see 'em. They belong to Stella."

I was pleading. "Maybe you don't realize it, but I'm standing in the shadow of the hangman's noose. Don't you see, there might be something in those letters—something that would— You got to let me see them!"

"Well—" He pondered the step. Then he got out of bed and crossed to a small table at the far end of the bedroom. He lifted the carpet and felt under it. "Here they are—"

I took them. There were three letters. I glanced over one page, and then a siren was screaming through my brain. They weren't signed. There was just the initial. I said:

"I think I've got a hunch, Pop."

"You mean—about who killed her?" His face paled.

"Yeah."

"You got to have more than a hunch. Proof—that's what you need. You ain't got proof, have you?"

I didn't answer him. I said: "You've got to make me a loan, Pop. Five bucks."

He hesitated, then reached for his trousers thrown over the foot of the bed. He pulled out some bills and peeled me off a ten spot.

"Thanks, Pop. How's your jalopy fixed for gas?"

He looked up quick. "A few gallons mebbe. I ain't got any tickets though."

"Mind if I borrow it?"

"Well—the lights ain't any too good, Eric. But you're welcome to it. It's sittin' right out front."

I left him gaping after me. I hurried back outside, then I was running to Pop's car. It was a Pontiac sport coupe—'34 vintage. It started up just fine.

A wild, tingling excitement was all through me. I knew exactly what my course would be. I was going back to Frisco!

Ernest Medley was the man I had to see!

23

I remember I ran out of gas, about two hours out of Walton. I stood along the highway, trying to flag a ride. It was about two in the morning, and moonlight was dissolving into darkness. Four cars had passed—and buzzed right on by.

The ocean breeze was the coldest I'd ever felt. My ears and hands and feet were numb, and growing number. I thought they must be frozen. I kept stomping around on the pavement, working my arms to stir up circulation.

Finally there were headlights again. When they got closer I saw they belonged to a truck. This time I stood in the middle of the road waving my hands like wild.

It was a gasoline truck. The driver said he was going two hundred miles past Frisco. He was a big, flabby guy, his stomach resting on the steering wheel. He said he was sure as hell glad to pick me up. He said he'd fallen asleep at the wheel three times already tonight and woke up just in time before he collided. And once he almost hit a telephone pole. He laughed like it was funny and told me he was carrying two thousand gallons of gas in the tank. I knew then that any sleep I had in view was out of the question. I had to talk fast and loud to keep this guy on his toes.

After a while we both got hungry. We stopped at a truck driver's haven and ordered doughnuts and java from a sleepy little Greek who kept yawning in our faces.

Back on the road, the guy got to talking my ear off—all about the war. He said Germany would collapse within three months and then it'd take another year to get the Japs. I could feel the warmth of the motor, and my eyes getting heavier. The next thing I knew he was shaking me.

"Wake up," he said. "It's ten bells. We're almost to Frisco."

He let me out at the edge of town. I thanked him and hoofed it back down to Market Street. The traffic was thick, and pedestrians were hurrying through the foggy morning mist.

After asking a half dozen people I found the Ebell Club. It was a modern, gray, flat building with lawn all around it. The guy behind the information desk told me Madley's engagement ran out last night.

"But maybe he's still at the Pixley Hotel," he added. "That's where he's been staying."

I knew if Madley had packed up and moved on it only meant I'd have to catch up with him. After inquiring some more, I found the Pixley Hotel. The desk clerk told me Madley was still there. He was checking out at noon. I'd made it by the skin of my teeth. After asking my name and plugging in at the switchboard, the clerk turned back to me:

"What's it in regard to?"

"A matter of life and death," I said.

He talked through the receiver and finally told me to go on up to room 412.

I took the elevator.

At 412, I rang the bell. The door opened right away and Madley stood before me in a checked robe, holding a cigar between two fat fingers. He looked calm and rested. His pudgy face and bald head shone like a billiard ball.

"Come inside," he said in a jovial way.

I went past him. I sat down on the sofa.

He took a long drag on the cigar, then he said:

"What can I do for you?"

I told him.

24

Afterwards, they told me how it happened.
All day long the sign sat out in front of Walton's city hall. It read:

> Tonight Only — 8 o'clock
> Return Engagement — By Popular Demand
> ERNEST MADLEY — SPIRITUAL MEDIUM

Then in screaming red letters:

> *I will bring you a message from Stella Flint!*

Pamphlets were mailed to every address in town. Word spread like wildfire. Even the cops at the jailhouse came around in front and kidded each other about the sign. In the shops and on the streets and even over back yard fences, people talked about the same thing: if Madley could bring a message from the murdered girl, why couldn't he find out for sure who killed her!

So at eight o'clock the hall was jammed. At ten minutes past there wasn't even standing room. The police department reserved an entire row up front—without paying a cent—and the cops straggled in slowly. Judd and the sheriff came in last and sat in the cop's row.

The Mexican was there, handcuffed to one of the cops. They were still holding him.

Dave Atkins stood in the back, close to the door. They said he was still a sorry-looking sight, haggard, with a bandage over one corner of his mouth.

Clara Barkley came in early, alone, and sat in the back. They said she kept staring ahead without a flicker of expression.

And Pop Elliot sat near the front—all slicked up in a light gray suit. He sat quietly and every once in a while he'd dab a handkerchief to his eyes.

When the house lights finally dimmed, a shiver went through the audience. They said you could feel it. There was silence for a good minute, and then the purple lights shone through the curtains.

The zombie assistant came out, made his lengthy introductory speech, asked for full co-operation. He stressed it even more this time. He left the stage, and then the curtains opened slowly, revealing the bare stage, the table and chair.

Madley came out and sat for several minutes muttering the communicable words. Then with arms outstretched, he walked up to the front of the stage.

A dead silence swept through the room. Madley tapped one middle finger to his forehead and spoke:

"The spirit of—"

Someone gasped.

"—Carl Latimer has come through. He wishes word with Charles Latimer, or friends or relatives."

The audience caught its breath. There was a long silence. At last a thin, middle-aged woman stood:

"I knew Carl Latimer," she said in a tight, low voice. "I knew both brothers. But Charles was drafted into the Army—several months ago—"

Madley tapped his forehead. He mumbled with closed eyes. Then in a groping tone: "Carl has been on a journey, far away. Now that he's back he's unable to locate Charles. Can anyone assist him? Does anyone here know the whereabouts of Charles Latimer?"

The thin woman got to her feet again. "The last I heard he was in England—in the Air Corps."

Again Madley mumbled to the spirits, in the language of the lemures. When that was settled he called out another name. He called several names and gave several messages from the deceased. He kept his audience spellbound. They sat fascinated and awed, hanging on to his every movement, his every word.

Suddenly he was tapping his forehead again. His face contorted. "There is the voice of—" His tone grew alarmed. "—*a girl!* She is trying very hard to get through—"

A quickening tension ran through the room. Madley stood there perspiring, in the shadow of the purple lighting. His voice went up, sharp and vibrant:

"The spirit of Stella Flint has come through—"

Simultaneously with his words there was a white flash of light on the stage. With it came a weird crackling sound—like the noise when a fuse blows out in your face.

There was tense silence and suddenly a woman's high shriek vibrated and chilled nerves. The audience stirred noisily. Then people were talking in the rear of the room. Two cops got up and hurried back to see what the trouble was. A woman had fainted. The cops carried her out.

When all was quiet again, Madley went on:

"She wishes word with—" He broke off. He mumbled quickly in the spirit language. *"—with Dudley Clark—"*

"That's the sheriff!" someone whispered.

The sheriff stood up. He was tall and lean and at this moment he was pale, his face drained white.

"I'm Dudley Clark," he blurted.

Madley's words echoed through the hushed room. "Her request is quite unusual— She wishes to—" Again he mumbled indistinguishably. His eyes flicked open. *"Stella Flint wishes to name the person who murdered her—"*

You couldn't hear a breath in the room. The purple lights paled and flickered too bright and paled again—into darkness. The room was pitch black. Then the purple lights flashed on and off sluggishly. A veil of gloom hovered in the air. The audience felt a cold gust of wind. Then there was the high-pitched, soft voice, seeming to come from the ceiling. It wasn't human, they said, but more like an anguished wail.

Hearts stood still.

Pop's face was white in the purple glare of the room. Clara was bent forward in her seat, holding one hand on her forehead. Atkins chewed nervously on a fingernail, and the little Mexican kept gasping, *"Madre de Dios!"* and crossing himself. They said even the cops were entranced. Judd sat there slumped down in his seat. You could hear his heavy breathing.

The purple lights kept fluttering. There was a soft tempest of noise from somewhere. It floated through the overcast room—like the intensified sound of a moth beating its wings against a bright light.

Then the voice came again—thin, feminine and ethereal:
"You didn't mean to kill me, did you?"
Madley stood as though hypnotized.
"You hit me, but you forgot you were wearing the ring, didn't you, Mark?"
Heads turned to each other in the audience. "Mark?" they asked. "Mark?"
The sheriff turned to Judd with a dazed, bewildered expression. Judd sprang to his feet, sweat forming slowly on his skin. His lids lowered, his face shook in rage. "What is this? What the hell *is* this?"
The voice came again, accurate and piercing:
"When you were waiting in the shadows of the rooming house you didn't intend to kill me, did you? I told you I'd go away with you, Mark—and we went to the restaurant to talk about it. But you shouldn't have struck me when I said I'd changed my mind!"
Judd's thick lips were white and trembling. "This is a trick!" he shouted. "All fake! Arrest this man!" He turned to the cops. "Arrest him!"
"You shouldn't have killed me, Mark. You said you loved me. You said it in all your letters. You bought me jewelry and said—"
"Stop it!" Judd whirled around to the sheriff. His eyes were bulging. "I say stop it! Stop that voice! Arrest him I say!"
The sheriff stood mutely with his mouth open. The purple lights flickered and sputtered.
"The ring hit me on the temple, Mark. The right temple. It still hurts. You haven't washed all the blood off the ring. If the police will examine it they'll find traces of my blood—"
The audience was on its feet, milling in the aisles, watching Judd and the cops. They couldn't understand it. They didn't know who Mark was. Except Pop of course, and the cops and Clara and Atkins.
"Mark!" the voice screamed. "It was Mark!"
The house lights flashed on.
Judd was waving his hands at Madley in wild frenzy, saliva drooling down the corners of his mouth. He was breathing so hard he could scarcely get the words out: "I've had enough of this! Everybody knows this is a trick. If it isn't, let us see her!" He

wheezed out a laugh. "Yeah—*tell her to let us see her!*" He turned to the sheriff. "Arrest him! Don't just stand there!" He pointed a shaky finger at Madley. "He's a ventriloquist! He can talk like a woman. That wasn't Stella's voice any more than—" He broke off. "It was *his* voice." He saw the cop's motionless, grim faces. His lips trembled. He threw up his hands in exhausted disgust, then he turned and hurried down the aisle, out the door.

No one stopped him. The cops stood as though paralyzed, with incredulous expressions. Then as if something had popped inside each one, they made a dash for the door.

The cops found him in his office at the jailhouse. His face was ashen and ghastly. He was standing behind his desk and the ring was off his finger, lying on the blotter pad. He kept staring at it.

The sheriff came in out of breath—Madley and his assistant close behind. Everybody stood there with long faces. Every pair of eyes in the room was on Judd.

"If you'll get somebody to take it down," Judd wheezed, "I'll dictate my confession—"

One of the cops got a pencil and paper. Judd started out in a low, dead voice:

"I thought I had a chance with her. I never gave up hope until—"

I wasn't there when it happened. I was in Madley's hotel room in Walton, pacing back and forth, smoking cigarettes one after another. I remember the tap on the door. I hurried over and admitted Madley's zombie assistant.

"It worked!" he said excitedly. "Ernest's over at the courthouse with the sheriff. They want you to come over—"

I was at the City Hall in three minutes flat. I saw the Plymouth out in front. The cops had retrieved it. I was in the sheriff's room when the cops brought in Judd's confession. I was there swallowing the dryness out of my throat. It was hard to believe yet that my plan had worked.

Some more cops came in, then Madley had the floor.

He was strutting around the room, still wiping the perspiration from his forehead. He said:

"That was the greatest publicity stunt anybody ever dreamed

up!"

The guys looked at each other.

A little cop spoke up: "Publicity? You mean—it *wasn't* her voice?"

"Of course not," the sheriff said.

Madley nodded. "That's quite right. Stanton here coached me on what to say." His eyes came up quick. "Not that I'm a fake—"

"Oh, no...." I said.

Madley ignored me. "The important part," he went on, "is that Judd believed it was her voice. He wouldn't have if what I said hadn't been true. Before he could reason it out comprehensively he'd exposed himself."

"Yeah," I said. "At the time Judd was confused because he was sure nobody knew about him and Stella. If it'd been a cop accusing him, he'd had an answer. But from Madley—a complete stranger—it was like cold water in his face."

The sheriff nodded and shook Madley's hand, and Madley left. Then I was moving over to the sheriff.

"My wife," I said. "There's no use holding her. Could I—"

He smiled. "She was released a half hour ago."

I was hurrying down the corridor, out the jailhouse door.

"Just a minute, Stanton—"

I turned around and saw the sheriff behind me.

"Not so fast," he said. He was grinning. "I want some explanation. How'd you suspect it was Judd in the first place?"

I tried to explain it to him hurriedly. I said:

"I probably never would have if it hadn't been for the letters he wrote to Stella." I remembered I had them in my pocket, so I got them out and turned them over to him. "I found out through these that Judd not only knew her but also that he was in love with her and buying her jewelry."

The sheriff coughed. "Kind of funny he didn't get rid of those letters, isn't it?"

"He was sure they'd been destroyed," I said. "I remember once he told me he'd gone through all of Stella's personal things. Evidently it was the letters he'd been looking for. You see, he searched the restaurant himself and asked Pop if he knew of any other personal effects Stella had." I paused. "He was worried about the letters all right, but when he couldn't find them he was sure they'd been destroyed. But it so happened Pop had them. Kept them and never read them."

"Even so," the sheriff said, "even if the letters say he was in love with her and bought her jewelry—how'd you suspect him from that?"

"A number of things. The first thing that hit me was that Judd asked me who bought Stella jewelry, and the letters proved he bought it himself. That was when I first smelled a rat."

The sheriff nodded. I went on:

"It got me to thinking, putting pieces together. Once Judd was talking about Atkins and he said: 'I couldn't have pinned it on him if I'd wanted to.'" I paused. "Why would he want to *pin* it on anybody! That was funny talk for a cop.

"Then," I continued, "what really made me think Judd killed her—was the nature of the bruise on Stella's temple. I remembered what the coroner had said: 'She could have been hit with anything—one blow.' Well—that sounded like a fist to me. She was hit on the right temple, and look here—"

I raised my right fist and brought it up quick to the sheriff's temple. "See that?" I said. "I'm right-handed, and I would have hit your left temple. But Stella was hit on the *right* temple. So whoever hit her, with a pipe or whatever it was, was left-handed. Hell," I said, "it couldn't have been a pipe, like Judd tried to make out. It wasn't that kind of a bruise. It was too small for that."

The sheriff nodded. "You suspected Judd then, because he's left-handed?"

"Yeah. You see, I saw him grill Atkins that day. I saw those left-handed socks he featured."

The sheriff scratched his ear. "But just now when you brought up your fist you were standing right in front of me. Why couldn't Judd have been at her side or behind her, or anywhere. Maybe he didn't hit her from the front."

I shrugged. "That's what stumped me for a while. But that's how I first suspected him anyway. And the bruise, there was just one gouge. I knew that when Judd worked guys over he wore a glove—because a smack from a fist covered with pigskin is much more vicious than a bare fist." I paused for breath. "But with

Stella—in a fit of rage—he wouldn't have put on the glove. It so happened that was the very thing that tripped him up. I knew Judd wore a big ring on his left hand. I wondered if he could've washed all the blood off it. Maybe some of it had worked down in the crevices, maybe a trace of it was still there—"

The sheriff nodded. "It's possible."

"Sure. But hell—even without those letters I should have guessed it was Judd all along."

His mouth was open. "Yeah? Why?"

I explained to him then how Pop's words should have told me, when he'd said he hadn't known Stella was going away with somebody—so he couldn't have told Judd. How did Judd *know* that—unless Stella'd informed him. I should have known right there that she did know Judd—well enough to tell him her secret plans. And even before that, the first day I saw Stella dead, Pop said he'd told one cop I was with the F.B.I. That cop turned out to be Judd. Pop said: "I didn't know he was a policeman. *He came in here most every afternoon and drank soda pop!*"

Stella must've waited on him. I should have known from that that Stella knew Judd. She'd said once that she knew a guy with dough who wanted to marry her. It was Judd she'd been talking about.

I explained how I went back to Frisco to get Madley, because I knew somehow I had to corner Judd.

The sheriff kept nodding. "Why do you suppose Judd went after you so hard?"

"Because he hated my guts," I said. "He hated Atkins, too, for that matter. But it turned out Atkins had a perfect alibi. I fell next in line. If I'd failed the Mexican would have been number three. That's why he didn't release the Mexican."

The sheriff said: "In his confession he said he didn't mean to kill her. He struck her, but he didn't mean to kill her."

"Well, maybe—" I said.

The sheriff tried to ask me more questions, but I said I'd see him later.

Then I was hoofing it down to Palm Street.

25

I thought I'd find her with Clara. But I had to walk past the grocery store on the way, and I saw the light. It wasn't five seconds till I was up the stairs. I turned my key in the lock.

Emmie was sitting in a chair in the dining room, her hands on her forehead, her elbows resting on the table. I stepped inside the door. I could hear the clock ticking. I felt hollow in the stillness of the room. I closed the door behind me. She looked up, her face white and strained. There were tears in her eyes and her lips were working. She looked thinner.

Her eyes met mine, and I knew there weren't any words. I felt myself shrinking into the world's smallest louse. I tried to say something but the thoughts all started out at once. I was never so tongue-tied in my life. I didn't use any of the fancy speeches I'd fixed up. They were all lousy. I couldn't fake my way through. I said:

"I—just came to get my clothes. I won't bother you."

I didn't want my clothes, but I beat it into the bedroom, swearing under my breath, wishing I'd gone on straight from the jailhouse. Things were better with Emmie by now. There was just the scar. I had to come back and rip the scar wide open. I was that kind of a guy.

I reached in the closest and yanked down my clothes—my only other suit—the one I'd worn to the wedding. I pulled some ties out of the dresser drawer and stuffed them in my suit pocket. It was then that I felt the rice, lying along the lining. I swore some more and threw it across the room. A lump just stayed in my throat.

I got out my underwear and rolled it up in the suit of clothes. I was going through the motions of packing all right. There was an old newspaper on the dresser. I rolled my shoes in the first section, my clothes in the second.

I looked up. Emmie was standing in the bedroom doorway.

"I heard about Judd," she said drily.

"Yeah." I unrolled my stuff and rolled it up again. I didn't want to go. The thought of hitting the road again made me kind of sick. I wanted to stay there—with Emmie's arms around me. I wanted to hear her say: "*We have each other, darling, and that's all that can ever matter!*"

I didn't want to go anywhere. I was tired of going places. Sick of strange people—people who didn't care if you died tomorrow or lived to be a thousand. I wanted to stay right there with Emmie and hang up my clothes again and put my head on the pillow and go to sleep to wake up to find her arms around me.

She watched me unroll my stuff for the third time and said quietly:

"You can have that suitcase on the bed. I'll have no use for it."

"Thanks." I kept my eyes away from her. I got to my feet and began to stuff my clothes in the suitcase. "Nice of you to give me this," I said.

"That's all right."

Her voice sounded plenty washed up. I knew it was time to scram all right. Everybody in town was on to me now. Hell, she was better off without me. I knew when it was time to leave. Emily Post had nothing on me there. I might not know anything else, but that was one thing I knew, when it was time to blow.

I still kept my eyes on what I was doing. I said:

"Sorry you had to go through all this, Emmie. I'll get some dough somewhere and start the divorce—just as soon as I get settled some place."

"You're leaving then?" Her voice was emotionless.

"Yeah." I snapped the locks and picked up the suitcase, then I looked over at her. I saw that her upper lip was swollen, her eyes all red. "How come your lip's puffed like that?"

She didn't answer.

"If I thought those cops got rough with you, I'd—"

"They didn't," she said quickly. "I—I guess it's only from—crying so much."

I was choked up. I rubbed my hand down over my face. "You shouldn't cry, Emmie. Hell, you ought to be glad. You got to the root of your ailment. I won't be hanging around anymore." I managed to grin. "But you'd better get smart and get that dough out of my name. I might get stuck somewhere and get ideas."

She only stared at me. "At first I thought it wasn't true," she said tiredly. "At first I thought the police were making up things—to turn me against you. Because they thought I knew where you were, and they wanted me to tell them. But then they showed me the reports—the one from the Los Angeles sheriff's office was—"

"Yeah," I said, cutting her off.

Her voice grew flatter and more helpless:

"Then I *had* to believe them. I had to believe Mark Judd when he told me you weren't a spiritual medium. That you married me only to get my inheritance, that you'd planned on going away with that waitress after you'd—fleeced me."

She said it simply, without the dramatics. Every word seared through me—like I was being branded with a hot iron. I'd never faced my suckers before. This was something new. I started for the door. She stood there, and suddenly she laughed.

"The great love of my life! I was deaf and dumb. Even Clara tried to tell me. But I had such faith in you, I—" She broke off, new tears starting, her mouth quivering.

I tried to cheer her up. "Don't cry, Emmie. Hell, this is war. You've got to conserve everything. Don't waste tears."

She didn't hear me. She said:

"How you must have laughed at me."

"No, I never laughed."

She came closer. "How can I believe that? How can I believe anything? You're so good at lies!"

I cringed inwardly.

Her voice was bitter. "Don't you ever get mixed up? Forget what you've said and get all jumbled?"

"Sure I do. Sometimes. Sure."

Her eyes searched mine. "And now you're leaving. What other lives are you going to corrupt? Where are you going?"

Hell, I couldn't answer that one myself. I said: "Somewhere. Anywhere. It doesn't matter much, does it? Maybe I'll find me a special little world some place."

She kept looking at me. "Everyone wants Utopia. But no one can have it. We have to know people and have friends. People can't keep moving about. They have to establish themselves, be part of a community, decent citizens."

I nodded. "Sure. But I—guess I'm not made that way. I guess I was made to—fleece people—and keep on the move."

She shook her head. "You're so crazy, so wrong. Don't you know—you poor fool—that when you hurt someone you only get hurt? That when you give pain you don't give it at all, but it blocks up in your heart, so that you can't sleep nights?" She was crying again. "I feel sorry for you. You have to live with your own conscience—"

"Emmie," I said, "stop it. I sleep all right and my conscience and I get along okay—"

Her face set grim. "Then you're heartless, Eric. You have no feelings. You're hard and calloused. You're like a tooth that's good enamel, but decayed inside. You'll never be happy. You're doomed for something awful. The decay goes too deep!"

I wanted to tell her then—that I did have a conscience. I wanted to tell her how it gnawed at me and gnawed—until it almost drove me crazy and I had to come back and straighten things out—for her, how it was all for her!

"Eric," she said abruptly, "I loved you two days ago. I can't turn off my love like—like—" She couldn't think of the words, but her eyes lighted. "You came back here and solved the murder. That was a splendid thing for you to do. Was it because of me?" She nodded a little, like she wanted me to say yes. "It was, wasn't it?"

"Don't be simple. I'm not a jerk. I couldn't keep on going with a rap like that hanging over my head."

She nodded disappointedly. "It's probably the first time you ever told the truth—"

"Probably."

"But you could be truthful always—if you'd only want to. If you had someone you loved, to help you, to earnestly—"

"You talk like a music box," I said.

Her face got scared. "You don't want to change—is that it?"

"That's it."

"You don't want any help." She said it to herself.

"No. I figure I'm okay as I am. A little rough around the edges maybe, but if people don't like me the way I am, to hell with 'em!"

I saw the panic in her eyes. I tightened my grasp on the suitcase handle and made a fast exit to the door.

"Be a good girl, Emmie."

She didn't answer. I hurried down the steps.

26

It was two in the morning. I'd caught the Greyhound in Walton. Now we were cruising along the Coast Highway. The night outside was pitch dark, clouds lining the sky, heavy clouds, like it would rain any minute. Inside it was warm. Soldiers, sailors, dames, kids. Two girls in Navy uniforms keeping up a line of gab with the bus driver. Nobody seemed to notice that the air was so tight you couldn't breathe. Nobody bothered to open a window.

It was too warm in there all right, but the chill of loneliness was there, too. Like it always is. People all around you that you don't even see, and you'll never see again, and even if you do see them again you won't recognize them and Oh hell—

What did it matter. What did anything matter.

She was different though, wasn't she? She was the nicest I'd ever seen. Emmie. I'd never forget that name. I'd never forget her either. What was it somebody said about—sort of a theory: all the heaven there is is right here on earth. Well, I'd had a peep at heaven. It was too late when I saw it though.

This gnawing inside me.... I wondered if it'd ever stop. I tried to get my mind off her. I pulled out the dough from my pocket and counted it over. Pop's loan of ten bucks had come in handy. Two dollars left.

I noticed the driver had an eye on the mirror, sort of looking the passengers over. He was handsome, with a moustache and black curly hair and dark glasses.

"Hey—mister—"

I slumped down further in the seat and pretended to be reading a magazine.

"Hey—Joe—"

Everybody in the bus was ogling around at me. Hell, I had to look up. I saw the driver's eyes meant me all right. "You want something?"

"I sure do," he said. "I want dough. If you intend riding on you'd better be forking over."

"What the hell—" I strained my eyes out the window. "You mean we *passed* Santa Barbara?"

A spontaneous roar of laughter came from the crowd. Everybody laughed, except the driver.

"We passed Santa Barbara over an hour ago," he said.

"Oh, I must've been asleep—"

"Oh, sure. Well, you can start fixin' up to kiss me goodbye in about five minutes. I'm dropping you, Joe."

The passengers howled again. It was very funny! So goddam funny I wanted to remodel this punk driver's nose with my fist.

"Okay, okay," I said.

Hell, it never worked anymore!

I got up and got my suitcase down from the rack. I set it in the aisle, and I didn't really notice it till then.

Damn good leather....

Before I was through thinking about it, though, the bus was slowing to a stop in the middle of a town. I took the suitcase and got off. All the eyes followed me, and all the passengers were making remarks. Even after I was off, people at the side windows kept ogling.

I saw the name of the town. I heard the ocean pounding.

Queen Beach.

I wondered what it was going to be like.

A fine mist of rain was falling. It felt good on my face. I walked on, down the empty main street. Every store was shut up tight, pitch-black inside. Nothing was open. I hurried on and kept straining my eyes for a hotel.

I heard a car buzzing down the empty street. It pulled to the curb beside me, and I heard the windshield wiper working back and forth. I looked over and saw the Plymouth, Emmie getting out. I stared at her, my heart pumping like a diesel engine.

"Eric," she said. "Eric, Eric...."

That's all she said. Then she was in my arms and I was kissing her as fast as I could and holding on to her. I held her for a long time and finally she looked up and said:

"I tried to catch up with the bus. But I didn't quite make it."

I couldn't talk; I was that choked up.

She said, "After you left I thought about everything. I thought and thought and thought. And darling, I discovered something—"

"What—what is it, Emmie?"

Her eyes were bright. "You've changed. You're as good as you were bad." She laughed lightly. "Do you know something?"

I shook my head.

"I thought about the way you kept rolling up your clothes and unrolling them so you'd have to roll them all over again. And even when you put them in the suitcase you packed them over twice. You wanted to *stay!*"

"Yeah. I wanted in the worst way to stay."

"But you didn't! And it was for *me!*" She smiled again. "Darling, you were being noble—"

"It wasn't that, Emmie, I—" I groped for the words. "I—remember that swell reputation of yours and I suppose everybody knows I married you for your dough, and you see—the only thing you could do was to get rid of me."

She nodded. "It's pretty awful to have to live with that gossip, and they've started already. Everybody knows about you, how you—" She broke off. "But, Eric, if you *proved* to them it wasn't true. Like if you took a job somewhere, and—"

"What'd you mean?"

"Darling, after you left we had a visitor—"

"Yeah? Who?"

"The sheriff. And he was terribly disappointed because you weren't home. He said he wanted to talk to you about accepting a position with his office. He said—"

"You're not fooling me, Emmie?"

"Not a bit."

I stared at her. "But what do I know about—"

"You know all the angles, darling!"

"Yeah, so much about petty crooks."

"No, not that. Don't you see, if you took that job, well—it would sort of prove to everybody that—" She broke off. "I didn't go to church to believe that a man can't have another chance. You've *changed* and— Oh, darling, would you? Could you? *Could* you stay still in one place and be happy?"

It was the craziest feeling. I held her tight again and then I was bawling.

"I'm a pretty mixed-up guy," I said. "Let's take it from there.

Everything they told you about me is true—except they left out one thing. You see, I love you, Emmie. I didn't know the meaning of—"

She put her fingers on my lips. "I know. That was the part nobody else knew, but I did. You could have lied to me some more. You could have even stayed long enough to get me to trust you again—" She smiled, "—and still fleeced me. But you didn't. You left of your own volition."

We stood there saying things like that, and finally Emmie said: "Why, darling—it's raining...."

I looked up, and sure enough it was. It was three o'clock in the morning and it was raining, but in Emmie's eyes was the brightest sun I'd ever seen! My heart was like Humpty Dumpty: falling around all over the place!

So now I'm working out of the sheriff's office. We're still living in the same place—up over the grocery store, and we're not going to buy the house after all—not until I get dough of my own to put in it. The ten grand is back in war bonds.

About Judd—well, you can write to him in care of San Quentin—and there's no particular hurry: he's in for life. They threw the book at him—murder in the second degree. Even the smart New York attorney Judd hired couldn't pull strings. What made it bad for him was the fact that he was a cop and had fooled around murder cases long enough to know that hitting people in a certain spot on the temple can kill them. If he'd given himself up he'd gotten off on a manslaughter charge—but it was the way he looked around for somebody to pin it on that got him the permanent address.

And I'm busting to tell you about Clara. It's sort of a laugh. She's keeping steady company with a bus driver. He makes town every other day. She keeps waiting for him. And it must be all right—because she's looking pretty good—doesn't complain about headaches or losing sleep anymore.

As for Emmie, well, she's *terrific!* Aid I love her in the daylight, too. Which is an okay thing. I'm a lucky guy! You ought to see her now when she walks down the street. The guys all turn around—but they don't whistle—because I'm standing there.

THE END

 Film Noir Classic #1…
The Pitfall
By Jay Dratler

"Dratler's novel is darker, sleazier and less forgiving than the film it inspired. A brutal portrait of blind lust and self-destruction that out-Cains even James M. Cain, Dratler's *The Pitfall* deserves to known as a stellar example of 1940s American noir."
—Cullen Gallagher,
Pulp Serenade

"These are nice, everyday people that Mr. Dratler has tossed into his meat grinder, and you will find it difficult to pull yourself away until you've read the last page."
—*Knoxville Journal*

PRICE: $14.95
ISBN: 979-8-88601-008-4

PITFALL: 1948
Directed by André De Toth
Screenplay by Karl Kamb & William Bowers (uncredited) from the novel by Jay Dratler
Starring Dick Powell, Lizabeth Scott, Jane Wyatt and Raymond Burr

Stark House Press, 1315 H Street, Eureka, CA 95501
griffinskye3@sbcglobal.net / www.StarkHousePress.com
Available from your local bookstore, or order direct via our website.

www.ingramcontent.com/pod-product-compliance
Lightning Source LLC
LaVergne TN
LVHW021822060526
838201LV00058B/3481